Praise for *Beautiful Girl*

"In turns heart-stopping and heartbreaking, but ultimately hopeful, *Beautiful Girl* is the powerful story of one girl's search for what each of us wants: to be seen, to be known, and to be loved for who we truly are."

—Erin McCahan, author of *Love and Other Foreign Words*

"Philips writes with conviction, heart, and honesty. Her words slip off the page and into your soul, reminding you that everyone is fighting an inner battle that most people know nothing about."

—Jessica Stevens, author of *Within Reach*

"Fleur Philips has written a poignant coming-of-age story of a young woman who sheds her masks and finds true love and her truer self. Romantic and compelling, *Beautiful Girl* reaffirms our ideals regarding the redemptive power of love."

—Leonard Chang, author of *Triplines*

"Fleur Philip's *Beautiful Girl* gorgeously illustrates that beauty definitely isn't skin deep. Add to that a powerful first love and some meaningful self-discovery, and this book will find its way from the beach with you to a soft spot in your heart."

—Jessica Hickam, author of *The Revealed*

"This beautifully written book has strong characters women everywhere will relate to, and a huge twist that will leave you in disbelief. A fantastic coming-of-age story!"

—Kristen Hunt, author of *Blonde Eskimo*

Praise for *Crumble*

Young Adult Winner from the 2013 San Francisco Book Festival

Young Adult Fiction Finalist by the 2013 International Book Awards

Silver Medal Award Winner in the Young Adult–Mature Issues category in the Moonbeam Children's Book Awards

Young Adult Fiction Finalist in the 2013 Best Book Awards from *USA Book News*

"*Crumble* is a timely, powerful, and important book. Fleur Philips offers a deeply personal take on the gun debate and reminds us all of the deadly cost of intolerance. Hers is a voice to savor and to heed."

— Gayle Brandeis, author of the Bellwether Prize–winning *The Book of Dead Birds* and *My Life with the Lincolns*

Praise for *I Am Lucky Bird*

A General Fiction Finalist for the 2011 Book of the Year Award from *ForeWord Reviews*

"One of the most stunning and visceral books I've read on child abuse this last decade. It is so brilliantly and beautifully written I found myself holding my breath through many of the passages.... I highly recommend *I Am Lucky Bird* to all of my readers. Five stars.

— The Bookish Dame Reviews

"Philips's writing flows off the pages.... The story still haunts me in many ways and the images that filled my head while reading are not easy to forget.... I think Fleur Philips needs to be applauded as an author for adding special moments of beauty to such a tragic story.... This novel deserves nothing less than five stars.

— Roxanne Kade

"I read this book in one sitting, it is just so powerful.... Although the subject matter is dark, the story is rich and powerful. A must-read book with spectacular writing and a protagonist who has found a special place in my heart."

— Minding Spot

"This is a gripping story, and you won't be able to put the book down."

— Hanging Off the Wire

"I finished the book in one less-than-two-hour sitting—I couldn't stop reading it. Period.... It's hard to believe this is the author's debut novel! Lucky's tale will stay with you, and will make you want to share the book with everyone you know!"

— Bless Their Hearts Mom Reviews

"A deeply emotional book that would stay with me for hours after I put it down and for days after I read the last page.... Hands-down, one of my favorite reads in 2012!!"

— Chick Lit Central

Beautiful Girl

Fleur Philips

SparkPress, a BookSparks imprint
A division of SparkPoint Studio, LLC

Published by SparkPress, a BookSparks imprint,
A division of SparkPoint Studio, LLC
Tempe, Arizona, USA, 85281
www.sparkpointstudio.com

First American Edition, 2014
Printed in the United States of America.

ISBN: 978-1-940716-47-3 (pbk)
ISBN: 978-1-940716-46-6 (ebk)

Cover design © Julie Metz, Ltd./metzdesign.com
Cover photo © Arcangel Images at arcangel.com
Author Photo © Melissa Coulier at Bring Media, Inc.
Formatting by Polgarus Studio at polgarusstudio.com

For Kevin.

Thank you for your constant encouragement,
and for your never-ending love and support.

-1-

Clarissa sees Decker Bail before I do. He's with a group of his friends, about to walk into the Adidas store behind me. I know she sees something because her eyes get real big and she coughs on the sip of banana-blueberry smoothie she'd just sucked up through her straw.

"Turn around, quick," she says.

And I do. When I see Decker and the two other boys I don't recognize, I turn back to Clarissa and sink into my chair. I pick up my Jamba Juice cup and wrap my lips around the tip of the straw, but I can't manage to suck anything through it because my throat's closed up altogether.

"Did you call him?" Clarissa asks.

I set the cup back on the table and look down at my chest, my unnatural cleavage staring back. It's a product of the extra-padded Victoria Secret push-up bra Mom bought me. I didn't call Decker. I wanted to, but I didn't.

"Mel!" Clarissa snaps. "He gave you his number. Why didn't you call him?"

Because I'm not like you.

I want to say the words out loud, but I don't. Clarissa's my best friend. Actually, she's my only friend. Like me, she's an actress and a model. Mom and I met her and her mother, Juliette, on a commercial set ten years ago when Clarissa and I were both seven. Mom found out they lived just a few streets away from us in Brentwood, and Clarissa's mom had just hired one of the best tutors in the area—Elaine Orton. By the following Monday, Clarissa and I were being homeschooled by Mrs. Orton together. Ten years later, here we are, sitting across from each other at the 3rd Street Promenade in Santa Monica, sipping on smoothies.

Clarissa is looking past me now and at the Adidas store, her mouth working the end of her straw like she's shooting a Jamba Juice commercial. She drops her head a little and lifts her eyes, sultry-like. And she *is* gorgeous—five foot nine with long, wavy blonde hair and deep brown eyes. Even though we look nothing alike—I have straight brown hair and green eyes, and I'm an inch taller—we end up competing for the same spots in everything. Commercials, television, print. And we see Decker all the time at auditions. He always ends up going for the roles opposite of us.

The first time Decker spoke to me, I thought I was going to pass out. He has the most amazing blue eyes and ratty, bleached-blonde hair. He's a total surfer with a surfer's body—all tanned and thin, with a washboard stomach. We booked a commercial spot together where we had to hold hands and pretend we were boyfriend and girlfriend. I remember wishing the writer had made us kiss at the end, but I wasn't so lucky. We just held hands and walked away from the camera, laughing. After the shoot, Decker gave me a hug. He smelled like Downy and some kind of woodsy cologne. The next time I saw him was at a print audition. Clarissa was there too, and I introduced them, but Decker kept his eyes on me. Later, when he gave me his business card, she swiped it away as soon as his back was turned.

"Holy shit, Mel," she'd said. "He gave you his number. You gonna call him?"

I snatched the card back and tucked it into my purse. "Of course!"

Clarissa sets her cup on the table and stands up. She's waving. My hands tingle, and then go numb.

"Decker!" she shouts.

I want to smack her across the face, tell her to shut up, but I slide even further down into my chair instead, until all I really want to do is crawl under the table.

"Hey Clarissa." It's Decker's voice. He's standing right behind me. "Melanie?"

Clarissa crosses her arms over her chest. "Yeah. That's her." She looks angry, but I don't know why.

I push my chair back and stand, then turn to face Decker and his friends.

"Hi Decker," I say, my voice cracking.

His blue eyes hold mine, and I feel my legs getting weak as my stomach turns, like I've just swallowed a glass full of sour milk.

"I told her she should've called you," Clarissa says.

My cheeks burn, partly from anger and partly from embarrassment, and I drop my gaze to my pink flip-flops and my French pedicure, a tiny delicate flower painted on each big toe nail. Mom insists my feet always be pretty, just in case I meet somebody important in the industry who has a foot fetish.

"It's cool," Decker says. "Her loss."

I look back at him, but he walks around me and toward Clarissa without meeting my eyes. The two other boys stare at me. One of them looks at my legs, then up to my waist and breasts. He stays there for a second before looking at my face. The other boy whistles as he walks by me, close enough so I can feel the heat of him against my bare arms.

Clarissa giggles, and I want so badly to turn around and call her a bitch, but I don't have the guts. And she knows it, and later, she'll make some snide comment to me about how I'm always too nice to people, how I don't have a mean bone in my body, how if I don't grow some balls the world will walk all over me like my mom walks all over my stepdad.

"I just don't get it," she'll say. "Peter's this badass lawyer but when it comes to your mom, he's such a pussy."

It's true too. Peter's worshipped the ground Mom walks on since he met her at some Hollywood holiday party twelve years ago. He's an entertainment attorney, and he was there with one of his television clients. Mom was there with Kurt, my agent. Sometimes, I look at Mom and Peter and wonder how they ended up together. Peter's not ugly, but he's not Mom. He's my height with thinning gray hair, hazel eyes, and an awkward smile—he has a thin space between his two front teeth and when he grins, the right side of his mouth curves more sharply than the left. Mom's an inch taller than him with long copper hair and deep green eyes, and her smile is flawless—bright white, picket fence teeth and lips like Angelina Jolie's. Peter's also thirteen years older than Mom.

Clarissa thinks they hooked up because Mom was afraid that if she didn't hurry, she'd be too washed up to attract anybody with money. She was a model into her mid-twenties, then did commercial and television work until she accidentally got pregnant with me by some hotshot director who immediately dumped her when he found out. When I was four years old, Mom started dragging me to casting calls and auditions and photo shoots and movie sets. I don't remember ever deciding I wanted to be a model or an actress, but that's what I became. Mom told me I was born to follow in her footsteps.

I keep my eyes on the ground as I turn and grab my purse from the table, leaving my Jamba Juice cup there. I walk away. Clarissa doesn't say anything. Neither does Decker, but when I look back briefly—a quick glance at my sweating Styrofoam smoothie cup—I see Clarissa's twisted little smile, her eyes clearly focused on me.

I run to the parking garage and to my silver MINI Cooper parked on the second level. My fingers shake as I unlock the doors, and when I drop into the warmth of the leather seat, I let the tears fall, knowing there won't be anybody coming after me. Not Clarissa, not Decker, not even the other two boys who gawked at me like I was a naked lady on a billboard. They'd seen me before, but I don't know them. Just as I don't know any of the faces who stare at me when I walk by and who whisper when I pass. I'm a beautiful face to them, a perfect body, the chick in the magazine or on the television. And they think because I look this way I have everything. I'm a spoiled little rich girl with a pretty smile.

I look at my eyes in the rearview mirror. They're Mom's eyes—that same deep green like polished circles of jade. But I'm nothing like Mom, and even though I'm glad I'm not like her, I sometimes wish I were as strong as she is. If I were, maybe I would've told her years ago that I didn't like this life, that I hated Clarissa and Kurt and the other people I have to be around everyday, all of them superficial like they're living in a comic book.

I start the MINI Cooper and exit the parking garage into a mass of cars and people and bright sunlight. I think about Clarissa and Decker and Mom, and I wish I could be home with Peter and Zach, my stepbrother. Zach's mom died during his birth from an aneurysm. He was just a few months old when Peter and Mom met. There are times when I wonder what would've happened if Peter's heart hadn't been so broken when he met Mom.

I take 7th Street to Santa Monica Boulevard and turn right, heading in the direction of 26th Street and then home. I can't stop crying. I don't want to do this anymore. After an audition or a shoot, Mom and I sometimes go to a mall—the Beverly Center or Westfield Century City. Mom watches the way people look at us when we pass. Men, and even boys my age, will follow her with their eyes. I see them, and even though Mom pretends she doesn't, I know she sees them too. I know because she sways her hips a little more and lifts her chin a little higher.

We'll sift through stores, sometimes buying a new shirt or jeans or a pair of shoes, but we're not there for shopping. Before we leave, we'll sit and have a coffee in the middle of an atrium, Mom letting her eyes drift from person to person. While she gathers silent attention, I seek out girls my age. They're always clumped in groups of three or four, sometimes five. When I'm with Clarissa, she mocks those girls.

"Oh my God, could you be more immature?" she'll say.

But I'm jealous and overwhelmed with a sense of loneliness. I feel the same way about them that I do about Zach—that I want to *be* them. I want to smile and giggle and whip at each other's hair. I want to link my arms with theirs and stomp through the mall wearing a sweatshirt with the name of my high school on it. I'm in the television show looking out into the real world, and all I want to do is shatter the glass.

My cell phone chimes, indicating I have a new text message. The stoplight ahead of me is green, turning yellow. I put my foot on the gas. Another chime. I look down as I turn left, for just a split second. A car horn wails, long and loud. My body jolts forward and sideways as the other car hits the passenger side of my

MINI Cooper. The seatbelt catches, the airbag deploys. Glass explodes all around me.

-2-

I open my eyes to a bright but fuzzy ceiling and blink a few times until the fuzziness gives way to sharp white. There's something on my face. When I bring my hand up to feel my cheek, my fingers touch something smooth, but rough too, like the Zapotec Indian runner on the dining room table at home. I try and sit up, but there's a tube in my arm.

What the hell?

The words sit on my tongue, but I can't get them out of my mouth because my lips are pressed together by the stuff that's on my face. And they're dry, like I haven't had a sip of water in weeks. A door opens. I try turning my head in the direction of the sound, but it feels like my skin is ripping under the Zapotec Indian runner so I stop. From the corner of my eye, I see Mom approaching.

She walks up to the side of my bed, a man in a white lab coat just behind her. I realize now I'm in a hospital. She takes my hand in hers—her fingers are freezing. Hospitals are always so damn cold. I've been in a few. The first real time I went (having nothing to do with a commercial or a television show or a photo shoot) was when I was ten, not long before Peter's mother died. Mom and Peter and Zach and me went to see her after she fell and broke her hip. I hated being there—all cold and bright and smelly like a doctor's office. I remember being so happy when I left, and hoping I'd never, ever get hurt or sick.

The man in the white lab coat has thin black hair and dark eyes, and his nose is slightly crooked.

"She's lucky to be alive, Mrs. Kennicut," he says. His voice is nice—deep, but soft.

Mom's eyes are all puffy and red. Her mascara is smeared. She brings a crumpled handkerchief to her nose, but she makes sure not to smudge her lipstick while she wipes. I can never understand how she keeps her lips so perfectly painted, all day. Even when she eats, it's as though the Lancôme Rouge Sensation in Red Desire is fixed to her mouth like permanent marker on skin. Whenever she takes me to an audition, she uses her fingernail to scrape any lipstick residue from the corners of my mouth.

"After all these years of teaching you how to properly apply lipstick, Melanie," she'll say, "I just don't get how you always let it smear like this."

"What are our options?" she asks the doctor.

He crosses his arms over his chest. "Once we remove the bandages, we'll have a better idea."

Mom puts the handkerchief to her nose again. She squeezes her eyes shut. Her fingers have warmed against my skin, but her hand feels rigid like she's made of hard plastic, like she's a mannequin. She says something to the doctor, but I can't hear her. They both leave the room.

I turn my head to the right a little. Through the window, the sky is grayish blue with not a cloud anywhere. It must be late in the afternoon because it's May in Los Angeles. If it were morning, low soupy clouds—what the KTLA weather lady calls a "marine layer"—would be smashed against the outside of the window. I lift my arms into the air, carefully, so I don't yank the tube out of the right one. My left arm has just a few small patches of gauze pasted to my skin. The right is covered in a bandage from my wrist to my elbow.

I remember a car horn blaring, then tires screeching, then a crash. Not a small crash like a single glass plate dropped on a hard tile floor, but a massive crash. A whole box full of plates being thrown from a ten-story building. My ears were ringing for a split second, and then there was pain, and when the shock of the pain subsided, my shirt was soaking wet. My eyes were closed, but I heard people shouting, and later, sirens. Lots of them, swirling and spinning and looping like twirling ribbons.

The door opens again and the doctor walks in, without Mom. He touches my arm. His hand is soft. Not plastic. His fingers melt over my skin like hot fudge over ice cream—smooth and warm.

"You're going to be fine, Melanie," he says.

The doctor said I was going to be fine. Lying in that hospital bed, I didn't think he was talking about my health. But he was. There was no internal damage. My heart was beating, my lungs were breathing in and out. My liver and stomach and kidneys were intact. And nobody else had been hurt. The man driving the car that hit me had a few lacerations, but nothing too terrible. Nothing like me. What the doctor meant by "fine" was that I was clear of any danger of suddenly keeling over dead. What he should've said was, "You're going to be fine, Melanie, but you'll be ugly for awhile."

In my bathroom mirror is a reflection of a makeup artist's dummy. I'm a Freddy Kruger victim, but unlike the actors in the movies, I can't peel the rubber away when the shoot is finished. There's no soft, clear skin beneath the stitched-up ground beef. Just a red mess of torn flesh I can't get rid of. Not yet, anyway. I take some comfort in knowing there's a way to fix this, to repair the damage I'd silently wished for when I left Clarissa and Decker and the gawking boys at the 3rd Street Promenade. It's not the first time I wished to be somebody else, but this wasn't what I meant. Fortunately, Kurt knows just about every plastic surgeon in Los Angeles, and he made sure to have one of the most recognized call Mom and Peter. Of course, Mom took the call from Dr. Levington and made all the arrangements while Peter just sat beside her and listened.

Zach is standing just inside my bathroom door, his eyes glued to my left cheek like he's waiting for maggots to appear.

"Joanne says you're gonna have surgery at the end of the summer," he says. "You'll get your face back, Mel."

Even though Zach was just a baby when Peter and Mom married, he's never called her anything but Joanne. She didn't want him calling her Mom. And even though I was five when they married, I've never called Peter anything but Peter. Also Mom's request. It doesn't matter that Zach's not my real brother. I love him anyway. I know most seventeen-year-old girls who have little brothers or stepbrothers can't stand them, but I love mine. He's the sweetest kid I know—always smiling and sharing and saying nice things. He got that from Peter, but I also think his mom must've been a pretty sweet lady, even though Peter has never said anything about her.

"I know, Zach," I say.

I've seen the before-and-after pictures on Dr. Levington's web site, and in most of his patients, you can't even tell they'd had injuries. I'm not scared. In fact, I'm relieved. He told Mom we needed to give the tissue time to heal. He would schedule the surgery for late August or early September.

"But that's three months away," Mom had replied. "What're we supposed to do until then? There's so much work she could be doing this summer."

Peter didn't say much. He just nodded his head, but he kept his eyes on me the whole time, and he smiled his awkward smile. He always does that. I think it's his way of telling me he understands, without having to open his mouth and interrupt Mom. He doesn't do that with Zach. They're just buddies. They have a connection I don't have with Mom, but I wish I did. I wish she and I could just be buddies, but I think it's too late for that now.

"You need a haircut," I say to Zach, his shaggy brown hair hanging in ringlets just below his ears. I try to smile at him, but it hurts.

"Whatever," he replies. He turns and walks away. Normally, he'd stay and talk more, but I think he can't look at me for too long without feeling bad.

I face the mirror again and take a deep breath, hoping the extra air will push down the rising lump in my throat, maybe shove it back into my gut where it came from.

You're not going to cry, Melanie.

It's been three weeks since the accident, and although the swelling has subsided, the wounds are still red and fleshy and lumpy. I was given a prescription of Vicodin when I left the hospital. Now, I'm just taking Extra Strength Tylenol. But it's not the pain that makes me want to cry, or the ugly person staring back at me. I want to cry because for the first time in my life—even if it's for just a few months—I don't have to go on any auditions or shoots. Maybe, I can just be…normal?

-3-

I haven't been out of the house in over a week. Mom won't let me go anywhere, but even if she did, where would I go? For one, I don't have a car. Clarissa has volunteered to come and get me a few times since I came home from the hospital, but I haven't wanted her to see me, and although she's apologized nine hundred times about being an asshole in front of Decker, I'm still not sure *I* want to see *her*. The text message that caused me to drive through that red light was from Clarissa. She'd wanted me to turn around and come back because apparently Decker kept asking about me.

"He really likes you, Mel," she said on the phone last night. "I just wanted you to talk to him, that's all. Can I *please* come over? I really want to see you. I miss you."

I ignored the faint gnawing in my stomach and caved.

"Sure," I replied. "But you can't laugh."

"I would never do that," she said. "Pinky swear."

There's a knock on my bedroom door.

"Come in," I say.

It's Zach. He keeps his eyes on the floor. "Dinner's ready."

I sit up in my bed. Before he can turn and run, I say, "You can look at my face, Zach."

"I know," he replies, but he doesn't look at me. "I just—"

"It's only for a little while."

He nods, and then leaves the room.

At the dining room table, I poke my fork at the roasted chicken on my plate. Mom's sulking because Kurt has officially signed me out for the summer. I think she somehow believed I could still audition, that I could at least book some print jobs based on my body and use Photoshop to make my face look like it did before the accident.

"We'll get her right back up and working after the surgery," Kurt told her.

He sent flowers and a card a few days after I got home from the hospital, but he hasn't come by. I don't think Mom wants him to come by.

"You're looking a little pale, Mel," Peter says. "You should at least go out and sit by the pool tomorrow."

Mom sets her fork and knife on her plate, hard enough to make a sharp clinking noise.

"Are you crazy, Pete?" she says. "She can't be out sitting by the pool. She needs to keep her face covered."

"Can't she wear a hat?"

Mom clicks her fingernails on the table. Eudora had been at the house today cleaning, so the mahogany surface shines. Mom wouldn't even let *her* see me. When it was time for my room to be cleaned, she came and got me and hustled me into Peter's study, where Eudora had already been. I heard her ask about me, but Mom said I was resting. Eudora has been cleaning our house for ten years. I don't know why Mom cares if she sees my face. She's one of the only people I know who doesn't treat me like a piece of glass. Zach and I call her Auntie U. She brings us something home baked whenever she comes—cookies or cake or bread. They kick ass to anything Mom buys, even the stuff she pays too much money for at a bakery in Beverly Hills. She doesn't pay for the flavor. She pays for the decorations—pink silk bows or cubic zirconium hearts. The cookies are pretty, that's for sure, but they taste like glue.

Peter looks back down at his plate and spoons a bite of chicken and boiled red potatoes into his mouth.

"I'm okay, Peter," I say. "I'm not really in the pool mood."

It's what Mom wants to hear. I wasn't told to stay out of the sun, but I know it has nothing to do with the sun anyway. Our backyard is surrounded by a twelve-foot-high brick wall on three sides, so the only ways members of the Halverson or Spagletti families could see me would be if they placed a ladder on their side of the wall or if they climbed a tree. But I'm not going to argue with Mom. I never argue.

Peter smiles and nods. He has a bad habit of chewing with his mouth open, forcing me to briefly witness his teeth mash the chicken and red potatoes into something unrecognizable and disgusting.

Zach looks at me, and then back at his steaming pile of red potatoes, drowning in melted butter and salt. He won't eat them otherwise. "Are you still coming to my graduation?"

Mom's utensils hit her plate again. "No, Zachary."

I'd just taken a sip of water and nearly choke on it. "What? Since when?"

I've been looking forward to Zach's graduation ceremony since he brought the little purple and gold family invitation home several months ago. Even though it's just elementary school graduation, it's a right of passage. Something I didn't get to experience myself. One by one, each student will be called up on stage to receive a little scroll, signifying that first step from childhood to adolescence. It seems so small and insignificant, but it's not. The boys have to wear button-up shirts and ties, black slacks, and dress shoes. The girls are required to wear dresses or skirts. I took Zach to the Beverly Center after he brought the invitation home. We found pants and a shirt, with an awesome kid's tie in purple, silver, and black. I'd planned on getting him a bunch of graduation foil balloons to give to him at the end.

"You can't go, Melanie," Mom says.

"The doctor didn't say that." The words come out slow and quiet, even though in my head I want to scream them across the stifling dining room.

She picks up her napkin and dabs at the corners of her mouth. She doesn't look at me. "*I'm* saying it."

A bunch of hands are wrapped around my lungs and squeezing. Zach is poking at his potatoes with his fork—up and down and up and down—but he doesn't eat.

"Joanne," Peter says. "Aren't you—"

"This is not up for discussion," Mom interrupts. She rises from her chair, dropping her napkin onto the table.

The gashes on my face are burning, like they've just been doused with hydrogen peroxide. Tears pool in my eyes, but I squeeze my lips together and hold them back. Mom turns to walk away, but stops at the sound of the doorbell—a bizarre compilation of dings arranged to sound like the first few notes of Mozart's *Andante*. Peter lives for classical music, often hiding in his study for hours listening to Vivaldi and Beethoven, Mozart and Bach. When I was younger, he didn't spend as much time in there as he does now. Sometimes, he'll even stay in there long after we've all gone to bed.

Mom looks at him. "Are we expecting company?"

He shakes his head.

I stand up, grabbing the edge of the dining room table with both hands to steady my numbing legs. "I am."

Mom turns to me, her eyes wide and terrified like I've just told her there's a knife-wielding man standing at our front door, waiting to be let in to slit our throats.

She sets her plate back on the table. "Who is it?"

"Clarissa."

"Clarissa? What's she doing here?"

"What do you mean? It's Clarissa, Mom."

She's gripping the back of her chair, her knuckles turning white. "I just don't think it's a good idea for her to be here."

"Why? She's my best friend. I haven't seen her since the day of the accident. She asked if she could come over and see me."

I want Peter to say something, anything, but he picks up his wine glass and takes a drink, a big drink, instead.

"Can I be excused?" Zach asks.

"Yes," Mom says. It comes out as a hiss more than a word, her lips barely moving and stretched thin. Her jaw muscles are clenched as though she's grinding her teeth.

Zach takes his plate and his water glass and hustles out of the dining room. I'm waiting, but I don't know why. Clarissa is standing at the front door. Mozart's *Andante* chimes again, and I pick up my plate and walk out of the dining room. Mom's eyes are burrowing into my skin like parasites, but she doesn't say anything else. As I step out of view, I catch a glimpse of Peter wrapping his fingers around her wrist, but she yanks her arm away.

I set my plate in the sink and walk into the foyer. Before I open the front door, I look at my reflection in the mirror hanging on the wall next to it, the same mirror I've been doing a final "before-you-walk-out-the-door" check since I was six, not long after Mom and I moved in with Peter and Zach. But the girl staring back at me now is different. Ugly. Grotesque. My throat burns.

It's okay, Mel. Clarissa's your friend. She's here to help.

I grab the iron handle, push the thumb latch, and pull. I smile at Clarissa, but the smile vanishes when I see the person standing next to her. Along with my smile, the blood drains from my face, sliding down through my chest and into my stomach, then down to my feet where it seems to pool, pumping and throbbing, holding my legs in place even though all I want to do is turn and run.

Clarissa puts a hand over her mouth and looks away, like she's going to puke in the hydrangeas growing along the side of the house. But Decker just stares at me, and I think it's possible he's stopped breathing altogether. I hold his gaze, long enough for the corners of his eyes to droop, and then he bites his lower lip and shifts his focus to the brick pillar next to him, as though something beautiful has suddenly appeared there.

I shut the door, my stomach a swirling mess, my hand shaking against the iron handle, a stabbing pain in my chest like someone's just driven a screwdriver into my heart. And then I'm on my knees, crying so hard I can barely breathe, my tears like acid in the wounds on my face.

-4-

Mom's first words to me before I ran up to my room were, "I told you having her here was a bad idea." Her first words to me when I returned home from the hospital were, "How could you be so reckless, Melanie?"

I don't recall ever feeling the way I feel right now, like somebody's just stuffed my heart into a box three times too small, then jammed a thousand tiny needles into my lungs. Each time I take a breath, the needles penetrate further into the soft tissue. I wonder if this is what it feels like to have your heart broken.

Mom can be hurtful at times, but I've always passed it off as Mom just being Mom. She's angry about the outcome of her life. She should've been a famous actress, right up there with Demi Moore and Kim Basinger. Instead, she's my trainer—and my chauffeur and my personal assistant—teaching and guiding and mentoring me as I live out the dreams she had to tuck away. I don't take her behavior personally. I know Mom doesn't want anyone to see me because she's afraid it will leave a permanent scar on my career. It's not because she doesn't love me. She's just looking out for my best interest. But there's no explanation for what Clarissa did to me. No sensible reasoning behind it. She's done her fair share of shitty things in the past—the most recent obviously at the 3rd Street Promenade—but that pales in comparison to what just happened.

I'm lying on my back on my bed, the blades of my ceiling fan spinning around and around, and I want to believe Clarissa did it because she knows how much I like Decker and she thought it would be a cool surprise to show up with him. But I know better. She's jealous of me. She's always been jealous of me. My booking ratio is twice as high as hers, and I'm hired for most of the jobs we end up competing for. And on the day of the print audition when I introduced her to Decker, her eyes lit up, then narrowed to slits when he gave me his business card. I realize now she must've memorized his number before I snatched the card back from her. I wonder when she first called him. How long has she been seeing him behind my back?

My hands are folded and resting on my stomach and now damp with sweat.

Why didn't I call him?

Clarissa's always flirting at auditions and on sets, even with men twice her age. Mom says if she's not careful, she'll end up in a dumpster. But Clarissa's dad's a big producer and everybody in the business wants him as a friend, so nothing will happen to Clarissa. And she knows it. She also knew I wouldn't call Decker, and now she's made certain he could never like me. The vision of my mangled face will be burned into his memory for the rest of his life. He could never look at me the same, even after the surgery. I don't know what they did after I closed the door, but I think I heard Clarissa giggle—a menacing, malicious, hateful sound. Yet filled with triumph. What have I ever done to her? I've been her friend all these years—listened to her gossip, encouraged her when she felt down about an audition, hated certain people in the industry because she hated them.

I close my eyes, tears burning them. My face hurts. Every once in awhile, it'll feel like hundreds of pins are being poked into my skin, and when the poking stops, my cheeks and forehead are overwhelmed with the sensation they're being stretched, like cellophane being pulled over a glass bowl. Dr. Levington told me it means my wounds are healing. When the stretching goes away, I wait to see if I might feel the same thing inside my chest, but I don't. The pain there is deeper and darker, like poison in my blood.

"Mel?" It's Peter's voice on the other side of the door. He knocks lightly.

I sit up and scoot backwards until I'm leaning against my headboard. I bend my legs and wrap my arms around my knees.

"Come in," I say.

He opens the door slowly and sticks his head in first, like he wants to make sure I'm dressed, even though he knows I wouldn't have said to come in if I weren't decent. When he realizes I'm fully clothed and sitting on my bed, he steps the rest of the way into my room and closes the door behind him. He's put on weight in the last few years. He's always had a slightly protruding belly, but his stomach droops more over his belt now than it used to. Rather than choosing to loosen his belt, he just lets his gut hang more. I think it can't be comfortable for him.

He walks to my bed, sits at the edge of it, and places his hands on his lap. He looks at the van Gogh print on the opposite wall—*Starry Night Over the Rhone.* He bought it for me in a museum gift shop when he went to Paris a few years ago, then had it framed in Brentwood and gave it to me for my fifteenth birthday. He told me he'd take me to Paris the summer after I turned eighteen, and since my birthday's in January, that's not even a year away. He hasn't mentioned Paris since he gave me the print, but every promise he's ever made to Zach he's kept, so I'm guessing he'll keep his promise to me too.

I don't know what to expect from this visit. Peter comes to my room every once in awhile to ask about an audition or a shoot, or to find out how I'm doing with my studies. Sometimes, we talk about his job or Zach, but our conversations are never very long, and he always seems uncomfortable. Mom has never let him be a dad to me. When the silence between us lasts more than a few seconds, Peter excuses himself by saying he has a bunch of work to do.

"You finding time to do make-up work from Mrs. Orton?" he asks.

Mom's been picking up my assignments, even though Mrs. Orton offered to come to the house to work with me.

"A little bit," I reply. "I'm behind some, but I'll catch up when I start feeling better."

Peter looks at my eyes for a second, then at my forehead and cheek, and then at my mouth before he turns completely around and stands up. He walks to my desk, tucking his hands into the pockets of his khaki shorts. Thick black hair covers his legs. Zach and I used to tease him about being half gorilla.

He clears his throat. "Your mom wants to take you away for a few months."

Of course she does.

I shake my head and turn to my window. Puffy clouds litter the darkening sky, like a giant paintbrush dipped in white ink was used to make splotches on a hazy blue canvas. I overheard Mom and Peter talking the other day, something about how peaceful it would be for me to spend the summer away from Los Angeles. Peter knew an attorney who had a house in Montana. He was going to ask about it.

He turns back around and leans against my desk. "I think it'd be good for you, Mel."

I don't know how he can think anything for me. That's Mom's job. Peter just agrees with her, and that's that.

He keeps his eyes on the beige Berber carpet screaming clean from Eudora's recent vacuuming. There's a bald spot on the top of his head, barely hidden beneath wispy strands of graying hair. Maybe if Eudora could use the vacuum on my face, clean up the fucking mess I've made of it, Peter might actually look at me for longer than a few seconds. A month has passed, and I haven't heard those familiar words from him—words he's uttered in secret to me just about every day since he and Mom got married. Sometimes, he says them in the morning before he leaves for work. Sometimes, he says them at night when he gets home. But since the accident, they haven't been spoken. Not once.

You're my beautiful girl. Say it, Peter. Please.

He pushes himself away from my desk, his eyes still on the floor like he's been assigned the task of studying carpet fibers for one of his clients. When he finally looks up at me, he appears defeated—his lips turn down into a slight frown and his eyes are bloodshot, the skin beneath them dark and sagging.

"Gordon Wetherelt has a summer house on Flathead Lake in northwest Montana," he says. "Takes his family up there for a few weeks every year, but they've decided to go to Europe this summer instead. He'd planned on renting the place out for July and August, but I asked if maybe you and your mom could stay up there. Said he'd be delighted to have someone there he can trust. Isn't even going to charge us." Peter chuckles.

The puffy clouds have disappeared from the sky, wiped clean from the canvas, leaving nothing but the darkening blue. But it's not a clear blue. It's never really been a clear blue. There's too much shit in the air.

"Well, I have a bunch of work to do," Peter says. He stands still for a second, waiting for me to reply, but I don't. And when he walks away, I keep my eyes on the brackish blue of the sky.

The dream started a few days later. It's the same dream, over and over and over again. When I was thirteen, I had a similar reoccurring nightmare where all of my hair fell out. I'd wake up in a panic and run to my bathroom, terrified that when I flipped on the lights, I'd discover the nightmare was real. Each time I turned on the lights, however, my long brown locks were still there, caressing my cheeks, flowing down over my shoulders, assuring me I'd have no problem booking the next job that required a full head of silky, cocoa-colored hair.

The dream now is worse. In it, my face is the face I remember from before the accident—smooth copper skin, full lips. Not a blemish. Not a scrape. Nothing. I run my fingers along the surface of my cheek. There are no grooves or bumps. No pain. When I wake up from this dream, I run to the bathroom. I turn on the lights to the remnants of something that was once on the cover of a magazine, and all I want to do is go back to sleep, go back to the dream where I'm the girl who still has the face of an angel. Worse than this, though, is the realization that I don't quite understand why I want to go back. I hate my life, and yet, I don't know anything else, and this is what terrifies me. My whole existence is about the physical me—my eyes and lips and teeth and hair and skin and body—all of the pieces of me people want to see with their own eyes. And who am I if I'm not beautiful?

Clarissa hasn't called or sent me a text message since before she showed up at the house with Decker. There are moments when I want her to call, but this only happens when I feel like disappearing into the darkest corner of my closet, or when I wish a massive tidal wave would crash into my house and carry me out to the farthest reaches of the Pacific. But those moments quickly pass when I close my eyes and see Decker's face, the way his skin paled and how he turned to the imaginary spectacle on the brick pillar. And then I think maybe I should just hold my breath and sink to the bottom of the pool, and stay there.

Would anyone even miss me?

Peter might be upset, although maybe he wouldn't show it too much. And Mom would be devastated, but I think she'd be more angry by the loss of yet another dream than the death of her only daughter. I think Zach would be the saddest. I know sometimes he feels intimidated around me, like I'm some untouchable being he needs to be careful with, but when we're at home, away from the masses of people, we're just a stepbrother and stepsister. We laugh and play games. We watch movies and eat popcorn. The hours I spend with Zach are the only hours when I feel like a real person. For thirteen years, I've been floating through life like a character in a book or a television show, and I keep waiting for the chapters to end, for the episodes to run out when the story's been told.

It's Saturday, the day of Zach's graduation, and the house is quiet. I drift into the kitchen. After the ceremony, Peter is going to the club to play tennis with a partner from his firm, and Mom is driving to Malibu to have lunch with a group of her girlfriends—women who do nothing but spend their husbands' money on expensive clothes and jewelry and unnecessary knickknacks for their million-dollar mansions overlooking the ocean. Mom sometimes complains to Peter about living in Brentwood, how we should move to Malibu so she can be closer to her posse of Botox lips and fake boobs. It's one argument she won't win, though.

Peter's office is in Century City, and he already has to leave earlier and get home later than he'd like. Plus, he makes a lot of money—enough for our five-bedroom, four-bath house plus swimming pool in Brentwood—but not enough for a piece of Malibu with a view of the Pacific.

After his ceremony, Zach is going to the birthday party of one of his Little League buddies. I've been home alone a million times before, but for some reason this morning the silence hurts my ears and the walls are closing in on me. Luther, our cat, is standing on the other side of one of the French doors that leads onto the stone patio. He rubs his sleek black body against the glass. He meows, but when I open the door to let him in, he crouches to the ground, his ears flattened against his head. A low growl hums in his throat.

"Luther," I say. "It's me."

He looks into the house, then back at me, and then he darts across the patio and down the stone steps like I'm a frothing, snarling pit bull. I think about Decker's eyes—wide and terrified at first, like I was a zombie or something, and then drooping as though he was puzzled or maybe even sad. Luther reappears at the top of the steps. He pokes his head around the corner of the stone wall, his ears still flat and his body hunkered low to the ground.

I'd been upset with Mom the past few weeks for refusing to let me leave the house and for not letting anyone see me. And I'd been shocked by the suggestion we spend the summer at some guy's empty house on some lake in Montana. But now, all I want to do is run away, far away, where nobody will know me.

-5-

Peter reserved a private jet from his law firm to fly Mom and me to Montana. The four of us ate in silence this morning, but when the car came to pick us up, Zach started crying. He walked up to me, pressed his cheek against my chest, and wrapped his arms around my waist. The top of his head reaches my chin already. I'm guessing he's going to be taller than Peter.

"I'm gonna miss you, Mel," he'd said.

"Me too, Zach," I replied. I wrapped my arms around his neck and squeezed, at the same time struggling to keep my own tears from falling.

Peter gave me a hug too, but he was more cautious, almost distant. I think if Mom hadn't been standing right there, his hug would've been stronger and longer. He sniffled, and then coughed a little, pretending his seasonal allergies had kicked in.

The limousine. The private jet. Peter's feeling guilty. And there's absolutely nothing he can do. I sensed it when he came to my room last week to tell me about the house in Montana. If he'd been confident about me leaving, about Mom taking me away and hiding me from judgmental eyes, he would've been enthusiastic. He's always talked about how our family never travels enough, how Zach and I are missing out on seeing the world. We've been on two trips, all four of us together. Once to Walt Disney World when I was nine and Zach was four, and once to Cabo San Lucas when I was thirteen and Zach was eight. During both trips, Mom supposedly forgot to tell Kurt we'd be out of town. Two days into our six-day Florida vacation, Mom and I had to go home early for auditions. And three days into our eight-day Mexico trip, we had to leave early. After that, Peter didn't plan anymore.

The limousine drives Mom and me all the way up to the jet. When the driver opens my door, he smiles at me, but then quickly looks away. I have a silk scarf draped over my head and sunglasses on, but Mom tells me to cover my cheeks with the scarf so just my sunglasses are showing. She then hurries me up the stairs and into the jet while two baggage handlers tend to our luggage.

The inside of the plane is small with room for just eight passengers. There's one leather seat on each side of the aisle, arranged so they face each other in twos. I pick the first one on the right that looks to the front of the plane. It just seems more natural to look out the window at where we're going, not where we've come from. Isn't that the point of traveling? To be excited about seeing a new place, not dwelling on leaving the old?

As I fall into the soft leather seat, however, I realize I'm *not* excited about seeing a new place, and I *am* dwelling on leaving the old. Mom isn't taking me on a vacation. She's assisting me in running away, and not really just assisting me. She's actually orchestrating the retreat. Peter and Zach are staying home, getting ready for summer, and I want to stay with them, to be a part of what they do because I've never done it before. But now I wonder if they're glad Mom and I are gone. It's not like we ever do anything with them anyway. My summers are always filled with beach shoots and industry barbecues where models and actors and photographers and producers and agents all mingle around someone's oversized swimming pool, drinking and gossiping and trying to "one-up" one another with their cars and clothes and miraculous new cutting-edge diets. Peter and Zach go to the beach or the park or the movies together on the weekends, and Peter has barbecues in our backyard with Zach's friends and a handful of the guys Peter pals around with.

Last summer, I left one of those industry events early. I told Mom I wasn't feeling well, but I really just needed a break from Clarissa. She'd been drinking mimosas all day and started crying about a Doritos commercial spot she thought she'd been cheated out of.

"Fuckin' bitch's boyfriend's one of the corinators on the shoot," she'd slurred.

"Coordinators?" I asked.

She glared at me. "You don't care for a shit either." And she stumbled away.

Mom was near shitfaced by that time too, so she gave me the keys to her Cadillac and said she'd get a ride home from Kurt. It's how nearly every party ends—me driving her car home and her catching a ride with Kurt. On the other side of the pool shaped like a giant squid, Clarissa had her arms wrapped around some guy's neck like he was a man-sized teddy bear she couldn't squeeze hard enough.

When I got out of the car at home there was music coming from the backyard, and voices and laughter and water splashing, followed by the screams of some of Zach's friends. I walked out the French doors and onto the stone patio. A small crowd of people—about twelve or so—were gathered around the yard and the pool. One of Zach's friends did a somersault off the diving board and everybody cheered. Peter was standing at the barbecue grilling burgers and veggies wrapped in foil. When he saw me, he waved. I waved back, but I didn't join the party. I'd met a few of his friends before, at his office or at the club when I'd stopped by to see him after a tennis match, but I didn't know them.

I waited to see if Peter might actually wave me over, but he seemed confused. Then, he leaned to the side to look behind me. I shook my head and jingled Mom's keys in the air so he'd see I drove myself home, again. He nodded, and then turned to a man standing to his left. The two of them broke into conversation. Peter took a swig from his Corona bottle. He didn't look back at me. I went to bed.

Mom is sitting across from me. There are seven empty seats on the plane, but she chooses the one right smack in front of me. I guess that's how it's always been. If she had the choice, she'd sleep in my bed with me at night. Not because she can't stand to be away from me, but because it would keep her mind at ease, knowing I was there, ready to attack my next audition and maybe score a big role.

The flight attendant is a young woman, probably in her mid- to late twenties. Her skin is bronze, her lips shiny with gloss. She has long blonde hair pulled back into a ponytail at the nape of her neck. I cover my mouth and cheeks with my scarf when she turns to me. She puts her hand on the top of Mom's chair.

"Can I get you ladies anything before we take off?" she asks.

"I'd love a cup of coffee," Mom says. She's flipping through the pages of a gossip magazine she stuffed in her purse.

"How about you, sweetie?" the woman asks me.

Mom gives me a look that says I don't want anything, even though I'm dying for a Coke.

"No, thanks," I say, my voice muffled behind the scarf.

The flight attendant nods and walks away. Mom continues to skim through her magazine.

"She's not gonna be sitting next to me," I say. "She won't see my face."

"Okay," Mom replies. Without looking up, she says. "Miley Cyrus's boyfriend sure is cute, isn't he?"

Not long after the flight attendant returns with Mom's coffee, the jet takes off, so smoothly the coffee barely moves in its cup. Santa Monica and the coastline appear below us as we rise toward the sky, and then the buildings disappear as the pilot cuts right. Now there's ocean with a few boats scattered here and there, and in the distance, a separation of water and sky like a belt's been stretched across the horizon.

Mom is so absorbed in her magazine, it's like I'm not there. Every once in awhile, she makes a comment about something she's just read: "Did you know…?"; "Have you heard…?"; "Can you believe it?" She's talking out loud, so I think she's speaking to me, but I wonder if she's really just having a conversation with herself. Her old self—the one she wishes were in the pages of that magazine.

I feel sorry for Mom because I know how she feels—wanting something so badly but not being able to have it. It's suffocating. Out the window now, there's land below us—long stretches of squares in different shades of brown and green, like a massive quilt's been laid out across the ground. Central California farm country. Somewhere down there is a huge cattle ranch Mom and I went by one time when we had to drive to San Francisco for a shoot. We decided to take the car because Mom wanted to spend a few days in Napa while I was working. For a good twenty minutes while driving by that cattle ranch, she made gagging noises because of the smell—cow dung and pee and God knows what else. I didn't particularly like the odor, but I'd never smelled anything like it before, and the newness of it, the raw shock of coming into contact with something unknown, was exhilarating.

I bend down and retrieve my purse from the ground for my bottle of Extra Strength Tylenol. Dr. Levington thinks the pain will be gone completely within a few weeks, but right now my head is pounding. It's not caused by the lacerations on my cheek and forehead, but rather because of the knots in my neck and shoulders, a result of unknowingly sleeping all tensed up. Even though it's okay for me to have pressure on my face, when I'm sleeping, my mind doesn't tell my body this.

"Be careful with those," Mom says.

The bottle is nearly full. The label says there are thirty caplets inside. I took a couple of them last night. I stare at the white oblong pills for a long time before I drop two into the palm of my hand. I pop them into my mouth and wash them down with spit.

There's a gnawing pain in the middle of my chest, like a bunch of baby rats are nesting in there, chewing at the lining of my heart and lungs. The sensation rises into my throat, causing the muscles in my neck to contract. I swallow at the lump trying to wiggle its way up, and I squeeze my eyes shut, hoping the tears won't slip out and slide down my chopped-up cheek.

All I want is to be normal, but this isn't normal. My face got fucked up, and with that came a glimpse of the possibility of a few months of peace. Instead, I'm being carted off to a strange and lonely place, like a princess locked in a dark and distant castle, and in that castle, I'll have only Mom, watching over me and counting the days until we return to Los Angeles to make me beautiful again.

I pull the scarf over my face.

"You okay, Melanie?" Mom asks.

"Yes," I say. "Tired."

But I'm not okay. And Clarissa's not my friend. She never really has been. She doesn't care about me the way a friend is supposed to care. She cut me as deeply as the glass that sliced my face. And I'm not okay because Mom is not a mom. She's the ghost of a woman who disappeared a long time ago when she found out she was pregnant with me. I'm just a reminder of why she didn't want to be a mother in the first place. As for Peter and Zach, I think they're just waiting until they're free—free from Mom and her anger and disappointment, and free from me, the rope that holds them back from being a normal family.

I slump down into the soft leather, wishing it could swallow me and then spit me out of the plane, flailing and screaming as I plummet toward the shit-smelling cattle ranch on the ground.

-6-

I'm yanked from my sleep by the voice of the pilot announcing we've started our initial descent into Glacier Park International Airport. He's looped the jet around so we're approaching the runway from the north. I pull the scarf away from my face. Outside my window are the most incredible blue mountains reaching like giant, jagged fingers into the sky. There are thick patches of snow on their peaks, like the Swiss Alps I once saw in a *National Geographic* magazine.

"If you're sitting on the left side of the plane," the co-pilot says, "Captain Johnson and I are giving you a little glimpse into Glacier National Park."

I can't pull my eyes away, and for a brief second, I forget to breathe. I forget where I am, what I'm doing. I forget Mom across from me, her magazine now lying on the floor where it must've fallen after slipping off her lap. There's a plastic wine cup in the little cup holder below her window, empty except for a squeezed wedge of lime and melting ice. When I'd fallen asleep, she must've exchanged her coffee for something stronger. A gin and tonic, extra gin.

I want Mom to see the mountains—deep blue like the center of the ocean, their snowy tips glistening in the sun like a blanket of shattered glass—but she's sleeping, her head bent forward like a raggedy doll.

I touch her knee. "Mom?" She grumbles. "Mom?"

She jumps and swats my hand away. "What! What!"

I point at her window. "Look at the mountains."

Mom squeezes her lips together, then blows them out with a deep exhale. "Please, Melanie. For God's sake, I'm tired."

Her voice gurgles, as though the gin and tonic is pooled in her throat. She closes her eyes and drops her head back against her seat. I don't care if she misses the mountains. She wouldn't appreciate them anyway. If they can't tell her how great she is, she won't want to have anything to do with them. I'd rather keep them to myself.

The plane continues its descent, getting closer and closer to the green-and-brown-checkered valley below where farmhouses and cattle and horse pastures dot the landscape. As we near the airport, the farmhouses and pastures give way to neighborhoods, and then buildings that don't reflect the sun the way the tall, glass skyscrapers in Los Angeles do. These buildings are small and made of brick and wood, maybe stone and concrete. It's a city, I guess, but not like the cities I'm used to—Los Angeles or San Diego or San Francisco.

When the jet's wheels touch the runway, Mom's head snaps back up. She leans forward and retrieves her magazine from the floor. "Did you need something, Melanie?"

I pull the scarf back over my head. "No."

When we step off the jet, the air is cool, and the sun reflecting off the runway is so bright, I have to squint my eyes even with my sunglasses on. Captain Johnson greets us at the base of the stairs and hands Mom a piece of paper. He turns and points to a chain link fence in the distance. Parked on the other side of the fence is a silver Cadillac STS sports sedan with tinted windows—identical to Mom's back at home, only hers is red. Our rental car.

Really, Peter?

Mom and I hurry to the car while a baggage handler retrieves our luggage. He pulls the cart with our bags to the trunk, then turns and walks away.

"What the hell is he doing?" Mom asks.

By the time she gets out of the car to yell at him, he's disappeared across the tarmac. Mom stomps her foot on the ground and shouts something, but I can't make it out beneath the whir and whine of airplane engines starting and stopping. I smile before I get out of the car to help her load our bags into the trunk.

I'm sitting in the rental Cadillac waiting for Mom. She decided to stop at a grocery store on the way out of town, but she wanted me to wait in the car. I understand why she didn't want the flight attendant to see me. The woman lives in Los Angeles. She might know somebody who knows somebody, and suddenly word is out that Melanie Kennicut's face is more disfigured than what rumors indicated. But we're in Montana now, in a town called Kalispell that Mom says is about the size of Palm Springs, maybe even smaller. Nobody here knows me.

I turn the radio on. I find several country music stations, then one playing classic rock, and another with easy-listening tunes. Whitney Houston's singing "Saving All My Love For You." Mom thinks Whitney was the most beautiful woman in the world—smooth, cocoa skin, brown eyes dark and rich like coffee beans, and a smile worth a million dollars.

"She had it all," Mom said after the singer died. "Beauty, talent. What a waste she just threw it all away like that."

Mom says that about every famous person who died too young because of drugs—Marilyn Monroe, Elisa Bridges, Heath Ledger.

"I could've been there too, Mel," she said to me once. "But I wouldn't have thrown it away."

After she said it, she waited a long time for me to respond, but I didn't know what to say. Her eyes searched mine for something, anything. I just shrugged and said, "I know, Mom."

She snorted a little and walked away.

I turn the radio off just as two boys and three girls walk out of the automatic doors to the grocery store. They appear to be about my age. The boys are each carrying a brown paper sack. One girl has her hands thrust deep into the back pockets of one of the boy's jeans. She's wearing frayed cut-off denim shorts and cowboy boots. The other two girls are trailing behind the rest of the group, both sucking on lollipops. Their skinny white legs dangle from the frayed edges of their own cut-off denims, but rather than boots, they have flip-flops on their feet.

I hunker down in my seat as the group walks past the car parked directly in front of Mom's Cadillac. The boy walking alone looks in my direction. I pretend I'm watching the store, but with my sunglasses on, I can keep my head turned to the right a little so he can't tell I'm actually looking at him. He's admiring the car. Not me. He grips the paper sack with one arm, and with the fingers of the other, lifts the tip of his cowboy hat just a bit so he can see the car better. Little brown curls poke out from the base of the hat. His lips pucker into a small "o" as he lets out an inaudible whistle.

The five of them pile into an old Ford Bronco not far from where Mom is parked. The boy driving stops at the edge of the parking lot, then pushes on the gas, causing the wheels of the SUV to kick up small rocks and dirt before it speeds onto the highway.

The engine roars as the kids disappear down the road behind a cloud of dust, and as the dirty puff of exhaust and floating particles settle, I wonder where the kids are going, in that car, in those clothes, with two brown bags from a local grocery store. I want to go with them.

I'm definitely not in Hollywood anymore.

There doesn't seem to be much beyond the store to the south, in the direction the Bronco is heading. On the drive from the airport, we passed a string of strip malls and car dealerships, and retail chain stores like Target and Walmart. At Main Street, Mom turned left, and we drove through "downtown" Kalispell—one long, four-lane street flanked on both sides by shops and restaurants and bars, and a large brick and stone courthouse at the south end. We looped around the courthouse and drove another mile or so before Mom pulled into the grocery store parking lot.

Farther down the highway—the Bronco now long gone—is a spattering of low buildings, probably more retail chain stores and gas stations, and then fields of yellow grass and patches of tall, green trees. The hill to the west of the grocery store stretches endlessly to the south. It too is covered in yellow grass and dotted with trees. It's not real pretty, but the stark difference to the sprawl of cement and glass that is Los Angeles is nevertheless pleasing to look at.

Mom pops the trunk as she walks up behind the Cadillac. She's pushing a shopping cart with three brown paper sacks in it. I don't even try to get out of the car to help her unload the bags. She'd snap at me for stepping into anyone's view but hers. She slams the trunk and pushes the cart forward until its wheels are resting against the concrete parking bumper in the space next to ours. Not far from that bumper is a shopping cart return area, but

Mom doesn't bother pushing the thing back there, as though its distance from her is ten miles rather than just a few hundred feet.

I think I must've gotten it from my dad, even though I have no idea who he is, because Mom just doesn't care about these things. Or, maybe I got it from Peter, like through osmosis by simply living with him. He hates it when people are too lazy to put shopping carts in the return areas. He hates it when people don't pick up their dog's poop on the grassy area between the sidewalk outside of our house and the street.

"They think because it's not *on* our front yard, it's okay," he'll say. "But it's not. It's still where you and Zach can step in it and drag it through the house."

He hates it when people park in handicapped spots when they don't have a handicap sticker on their license plate. And he hates it when people don't let him merge onto the freeway when the traffic is bumper-to-bumper anyway.

"Is letting me in front of you *really* going to get you there that much later?" he'll say to himself, but he's actually talking to the person in the car next to him who's being a jackass.

I think Peter became an attorney because he wants to stand up for people like himself—people who hate this or that and are tired of getting stepped on. And yet, Mom is all of those people Peter hates, but he loves her anyway. He loves her so much, she's the one person he won't speak up to because I think he's afraid he'll say something that will make her stop loving him. As Mom gets into the car, I realize just how much I *am* like Peter. All I have is Mom. I can't let her stop loving me.

We drive out of the grocery store parking lot and onto the highway, following the path of the Bronco. There are a few turnouts where it could've gone that don't lead to a gas station or a farm-supply chain store or a self-storage facility, but down those roads are nothing but empty stretches of pavement or gravel flanked on both sides by fields of yellow or green.

I'm looking back at a separate highway heading east, a green sign posted before it with a white arrow pointing to the right and the word Bigfork printed in thick letters, when Mom says, "Wow."

I turn around to an expanse of blue-green water nestled beneath a mountain range. From the grocery store parking lot, it wasn't visible, as though it'd been hiding and waiting for just the right moment to show its magic. There doesn't seem to be an end to the water, and for a brief second, I think maybe it's an ocean. But it's not. It's Flathead Lake.

"It's the largest freshwater lake west of the Mississippi," Peter had said before we left, like somehow that information was supposed to make me feel better about going there.

But now I'm actually looking at the lake, and my breath catches at the sight of it. As the highway curves to the right, I notice Mom can't keep her eyes on the road, so she pulls into the gravel driveway of a restaurant made of logs and parks the car.

"Wow," she says again.

Something about the tone in her voice makes my stomach flutter, like a swarm of tiny butterflies has just come alive after lying still since the day I was born. There seems to be an obvious appreciation for the lake and the mountains that maybe she's never experienced before. Or at least I've never witnessed her experiencing it before.

"Peter couldn't have found a more remote place than this," she says. "This is perfect, Melanie. Not sure what we're going to do here for two months, but at least we won't have to worry about anybody seeing you."

The butterflies stop flying and drop like a massive ball of lead back to the bottom of my stomach.

-7-

Gordon Wetherelt's summer house is not what I expected. My impression of a "summer house" came from books I'd read—in one case, it was a small wooden cabin set deep in the woods with a thin, rocky trail leading to the water's edge. In another, an old model home with creaky floors and a tiny gas fireplace with a rickety slat staircase dropping to a sandy beach.

The house is not small, nor is it old. It's a two-story, five-bedroom, four-bath log home with floor-to-ceiling cathedral-style windows above three sets of French doors that open onto a massive stone deck complete with a built-in steel barbecue and outdoor kitchen. Beyond the deck to the west is Flathead Lake with those beautiful blue mountains in the distance—the Mission Mountains, I learned from a small brochure I found in the rental car's glove compartment. Not more than a hundred feet from the edge of the deck is an L-shaped dock extending out into the water.

I helped Mom unload the car this time—the closest neighbors on either side of the house are separated from us by a good distance, and by carefully planted rows of ponderosa pine trees and private wood fencing. From what I could tell, there wasn't anybody around anyway. When I stepped out of the car, I stood still for a moment, the silence so heavy my ears actually started to hurt.

After we put the groceries away, Mom went up the staircase to the second-floor landing and to the master bedroom—the only room on the second floor—and I found the guest bedroom off the main living room on the first floor where I pushed my suitcase into one corner. The other three bedrooms were decorated for Gordon's three children: *Star Wars* in one, lots of pink in another, and posters of swimsuit models and rappers in the third.

I walk out of the guest bedroom and back into the main room that includes the kitchen, the dining room, and the living room. A stone fireplace serves as one wall and stretches all the way up to the ceiling, a ceiling that seems miles above my head. I want to yell something because I know my voice will echo, but Mom is in her room talking on her cell phone, so I don't.

I step out onto the stone deck, but Mom's voice follows, and I realize it's coming from the master bedroom window. She must've opened it when she was settling in. I don't want to listen to her, so I walk down a short set of steps and onto the gently sloping lawn, then toward the rocky shore of the lake. The air is still, but tiny ripples blanket the surface of the water anyway and come at me. When each one reaches the shore, it makes quiet lapping noises against the rocks, and then disappears, only to be followed by another, and then another. I bend down and touch the water. There's a school of tiny fish not far from me, hovering just below the surface like a flock of hummingbirds frozen in the air. They float and drift, seemingly unaware of my presence. Then suddenly, they dart away, so quickly it's as though they simply vanished. A twig breaks behind me, and I stand and turn, expecting Mom to be standing there with her hands on her hips, but instead, there's a boy wearing a blue baseball cap and holding a rake.

I take a step back, my pink flip-flop sinking into the water, and then step forward again and shake my foot. My heart is racing, but the sting of the cold on my toes demands more attention at that moment than the kid with the rake.

"Damn," I say.

"Cold?" the boy asks, his voice carrying a slight accent I've never heard before.

He's a couple of inches taller than me, his skin dark. Not olive like mine, but darker. And not black, but brown. More like the color of the amber beer Peter sometimes drinks. His hair is black and long and straight, tucked behind his ears beneath the baseball cap and falling to just below his shoulders.

I look down at my foot. "Yeah."

"Too early still," he says. "Water doesn't really warm up until mid- to late July."

When I look at him again, he holds my gaze for a moment, his eyes dark and warm. And he's actually looking at my eyes, not at my cheek or my forehead. My eyes.

He removes his baseball cap and tucks it under his arm, then extends his hand to me. "I'm Sam."

At first, I can't help but just stare at his outstretched fingers, brown and dirty. He notices my hesitation and wipes his hand on his jeans, adding to stains already soaked into the denim.

"Sorry," he says. "Been here most of the day." He offers me his hand again, and I take it in mine, his calloused fingers rough against my skin.

"Melanie," I say, trying to keep my face tilted down enough so he won't be drawn to my wounds.

"Right," he says. "Mr. Wetherelt told me about you and your mom. Staying for the summer, huh?"

I nod.

"I tend to the place," he says. "Mow the lawn, trim the trees, take care of fallen leaves."

I can't tell now if he's trying to make eye contact or if he's staring at the gashes on my face because I'm watching his knees.

"You don't have to be scared of me," he says. "I'm an Indian, Melanie, but we don't carry bows and arrows anymore. I'm not gonna scalp you or anything."

My face warms with the rush of blood to my cheeks. I look at him. "Really? You're an Indian?"

"Funny," he says. He turns and walks toward the south side of the house and to a green garbage bin, then stops and begins raking at the ground.

I want to follow him and tell him I'm not afraid, that I'd never met an Indian before so how could I be afraid, that I was keeping my head down because I didn't want him to look at me, but my feet have turned into slabs of steel, and I can't move no matter how much I want to.

"Melanie?" It's Mom's voice piercing the air, yanking my legs from their frozen state, stopping the tiny ripples from lapping against the shore.

Sam turns toward the house. Mom is watching him. He waves, but she doesn't return the gesture. He looks back at me, and then continues raking. When I reach the deck and walk inside, Mom stays behind for a moment before she follows.

"Who's that?" she asks as I sink into the soft leather of the L-shaped sofa in the living room.

"I don't know," I reply. "Looks like a gardener, I guess."

"Did he see you up close?"

Yes. And he spoke to me, and he didn't even notice the scars on my face. He only cared that I wouldn't look at him because he thought I was scared of him.

"Melanie?"

"I don't think so."

She turns around and locks the French doors, then walks into the kitchen.

"Is spaghetti okay for dinner?" she asks.

I rise from the sofa and walk back to peer at Sam. "Yes."

He's moved closer to the lake, raking at scatters of leaves and pine needles and lifting them in small armfuls into the green bin, his biceps well-defined and glistening with sweat. He stops briefly to remove his hat and wipe at his brow with a hand towel he pulls from the back pocket of his blue jeans—jeans that are sagging a bit, either because his butt is too small to fill them, or because they're a size too large for his thin body. I'm not sure if I think he's cute. I've worked with enough boys like him—long hair and dark skin—but they weren't Indians, and they certainly wouldn't be caught dead raking someone's leaves, unless it was required for a shoot.

Sam tucks the towel back into the pocket of his jeans. He returns the baseball cap to his head, and then remains still for a moment, his back to me as he stares out across the blue of the lake, his hands folded over each other and resting on the top of the rake's shaft. I follow his gaze—water and sky and mountains, quiet and still. When I look back at him, I suddenly wish I were seeing through his eyes, reading his thoughts, feeling what he feels.

"You need to stay away from that boy, Melanie," Mom says. She's behind me. I didn't hear her.

I turn around. "What?"

"That boy." She nods in the direction of Sam.

I glance at him. "Oh…I didn't know he was still there." I turn back to Mom and shrug. "I was looking at the lake." I walk past her and through the living room. "I'm gonna take a shower."

As I reach the door to the guest bedroom, she yells, "I mean it, Melanie."

-8-

A week has passed and Sam hasn't returned. The night after we met, I couldn't sleep, but I think it was more because of my unfamiliar surroundings than anything else. I opened the window in the guest bedroom to wind blowing through the trees and water gently lapping against the shore. The sounds were so different from what I hear at home that at first I was scared. But after awhile, they lulled me to sleep. Every night since, I've kept the window open. There's the wind and the water, but there are other noises now too—occasional chirping of crickets, the snap of a branch in a distant tree, the call of an owl, the scurry of small animals across the leaves beneath the window. That first night, I was afraid. Now, these sounds are like a lullaby.

Mom has spent most of the hours of the days in the master bedroom on her cell phone, talking to her gaggle of friends from Malibu, or to Kurt, or to Peter. When she's on the phone with Peter, her voice is louder and heavier, but I still can't make out anything she's saying. The night before we left, Peter gave me a bag full of books he picked up at Barnes & Noble, so I've been spending the time reading, either in the living room, or in one of the Adirondack chairs on the deck, or on a blanket on the dock. Before this week, I can't remember ever reading a book just because I wanted to. Mrs. Orton assigns Clarissa and me a book to read every month, but they're never of our choosing, and finding time to squeeze in a page here and there with my schedule isn't easy. In just six days, I've managed to finish two of Peter's books, and because he asked one of the assistants at the bookstore to help him, the selections are better than anything Mrs. Orton ever assigned.

Mom has driven to Kalispell twice since we arrived, for groceries and to a Blockbuster to pick up movies. During those hours when she was gone, I walked around the property, hoping Sam might suddenly show up before she got back, but he didn't. At night, Mom and I watch movies together or just something on regular television, but during the commercial breaks, she makes comments about how much money we're losing having to wait so long for my surgery. I don't respond, and after awhile she just goes to bed without saying another word.

I'm up earlier than she is again this morning. She slept in the past four days, yesterday all the way to ten o'clock. At home, she never sleeps past 6:30. This is mostly because Peter is always up at six. But I also know Mom's whole life revolves around my schedule, and one of the first things she does when she gets up is check the breakdowns to make sure Kurt isn't missing something I might be right for. Most of the time, he doesn't, but it's happened once or twice, and Mom refuses to let it happen again.

There are no breakdowns to check here. There are no early call times or last-minute audition notices, and I think the realization of this—as much as Mom hates it—has finally settled. I think she must be exhausted from thirteen years of watching over me, of critiquing everything I eat and drink, of hustling me around from place to place and smiling for me when I have no strength left to do it for myself. When she came down the stairs yesterday in her robe and slippers, her hair tousled from sleep, her face void of any makeup, I wanted to give her a hug. I'd made coffee, and she actually smiled at me and said thanks. But I didn't give her a hug. I'm not sure I know how.

I look at myself in the mirror in the guest bathroom. The wounds are no longer so ugly. There's a scar across my forehead that starts from the top right and runs jagged down to the tip of my left eyebrow where it stops. From the center of it, another scar runs straight across and stops at my left temple. Below my right eye is a scar that runs from the edge of my nose, down across my cheek, stopping at my jawline. They are still fleshy and red, but the gashes seem to be healing at the pace Dr. Levington had hoped. I'm trying to recognize the person beneath the scars. I smile, and the one on my cheek moves as though it has a life of its own, like it's not really a part of my skin, but more like an object that's been glued there. For a second, I want to laugh.

From somewhere outside, a lawn mower rumbles to life.

Sam?

I hustle out of the bathroom and into the living room. The sound is coming from the front yard. An old red pickup truck is parked in the driveway, a trailer hitched to the back. Beyond the truck, between the two large maples trees in the front yard, Sam is sitting on a riding lawn mower, the same blue baseball hat covering his head, his hair pulled back in a ponytail at the nape of his neck.

There's a tightening in the very pit of my stomach, the twisting of a knot so strong the skin on my legs tingles. Maybe it's because I haven't seen another face besides Mom's in a week. Maybe it's because nobody has called me on my cell phone, even though the only people who call me are Clarissa, Kurt, Peter, and Mrs. Orton. Or maybe it's because I'm still trying to get over Decker, even though there's really nothing to get over. He gave me a hug once, and his business card. I'm not sure it's any of these things, though. When Sam spoke to me, he spoke to *me*—not my eyes or my lips or my breasts or my legs. He wasn't trying to figure out if I'd look good in his magazine, if I'd move my hips the right way for his commercial, if I'd say my lines correctly in his movie. And he didn't cringe at the gashes on my face. For all he knows, they've always been there. In fact, he didn't seem to notice them at all.

I rush back into the guest bedroom and slip into a pair of jeans and a T-shirt. I pull my hair into a topknot bun on my head and wash my face with the cleanser the doctor prescribed for me. It still burns a little in places, but the pain disappears quickly when I rinse it away with cold water. I apply a thin layer of prescription moisturizer, and then brush my teeth. When I turn the water off, the rumbling of the lawn mower is just outside the bathroom window. Sam is in the backyard now, but the master bedroom window is above mine. I don't want Mom to wake up. Not yet. Not before I've had a chance to talk to Sam.

I slip into my flip-flops and run through the living room and out the French doors. The lawn mower is across the yard, near the fence separating the Wetherelt's property from the north neighbor. Sam's moving toward the water's edge where I'm guessing he'll then turn the machine in my direction and head back up. It's what our landscaper at home does when he's mowing our lawn—a careful pattern of horizontal lines that makes the yard look like a striped green rugby sweater when he's done.

When Sam turns in my direction, I wave my hands in the air as I run toward him. He stops the machine and stares at me for a second, then turns the engine off and drops his arms over the steering wheel so his fingers dangle over the edge. He smiles as I near him, and that same twisting-knot sensation explodes inside my stomach. I stop in front of the lawn mower, but I don't know what to say. I look at the master bedroom window instead, and then back at Sam.

"You don't want to wake her up," I say, my voice rushing out of me like air from a popped tire.

He lifts the brim of his hat with the back of one hand.

"I start at eight," he says. "Too early for you, huh? Was for Mike too, Mr. Wetherelt's oldest son, so I started coming in the afternoons. Thought since you guys were here instead, it'd be okay to get an early start. Lets me get back to my dad before he breaks into the liquor cabinet." Sam winks at me.

"Uh…it's fine," I say. "To come early. It's just…she's been sleeping in."

He looks around at the yard. "Guess I could leave it here and come back later. I only live about five miles from here."

"No. It's okay, really. You don't have to come back later." My throat is closing in on itself. I cough.

"You okay?" Sam asks.

The painted flowers on my big toe nails distract me. "Yeah. I just…wanted to talk to you before…before she gets up."

He slumps back in the seat of the lawn mower and crosses his arms over his chest. "Ahhh, doesn't want you talking to the Indian kid. I get it."

"That's not it," I reply. "She doesn't know you're an Indian. I don't think she does, anyway. She doesn't want me talking to anybody."

Sam straightens back up and wraps his fingers around the steering wheel. "And why not? You a troublemaker? Is that why you're here? To keep you from making more trouble where you're from?"

A troublemaker?

"No. I'm…." I look at the master bedroom window again, and then back at Sam. I smile. "Yeah. That's it. I'm a troublemaker."

He narrows his eyes at me. "Uh-huh."

I touch the scar on my forehead. "I was in a fight. At my school."

Sam shakes his head. "Mr. Wetherelt told me you were in a car accident. Said you were a teen actress and that you're getting plastic surgery at the end of the summer, that your mom wanted to get you out of the city for awhile."

My cheeks are burning.

"Nice try, though," Sam says. "Most of the places around here are owned by rich Californians." He points to the property to the north, the house nearly invisible behind a row of thick pine trees. "That place belongs to the guy who owns half the buildings in Los Angeles. Comes up here to get away." Sam smiles. "A teenage troublemaker who gets sliced at school? Not a chance. A disgruntled Hollywood movie star? Sure."

The tight knot in my stomach fades, replaced by a writhing bowl of snakes, twisting and squirming. I step away from the lawn mower and walk back toward the house. It doesn't matter what I do now. Sam knows who I am, where I came from. He didn't stare at my face when he first met me because he knew what had happened. He expected to see a Halloween mask when I turned around. And now I realize he's no different than anybody else I know—sneaky and conniving and willing to say anything to get what he wants.

"Melanie?"

I don't turn around.

"Melanie?" Sam says again, only now he's right behind me. His fingers wrap around my forearm. I stop. "I'm really sorry. I didn't mean anything by it."

I resist the urge to keep walking and instead turn around to face him. His dark eyes hold mine.

"Why did you lie?" he asks.

"I'm not a disgruntled Hollywood movie star," I reply.

He releases his grip on my arm. "I know. And I'm sorry. That wasn't fair."

"Why did *you* lie?" I ask.

He shrugs. "I don't know. I guess I was just hoping it wasn't true. What Mr. Wetherelt told me. I take care of a lot of these places, Melanie. I know these people and their kids. I watched you when you were at the water, and…it felt like you were different."

The snakes stop squirming around inside my stomach. Sam lifts his hand to my face and touches the scar on my forehead. I start to pull away, but stop and close my eyes instead, letting the warmth of his fingers kiss my skin. He gently traces the scar from my hairline to the top of my eyebrow. My body sways, and I take a short step toward him. When I open my eyes, my face is just inches away from his. I'm dizzy.

He moves his hand to the scar on my cheek, but instead of tracing it with his fingers, he places his entire palm over it. His thumb comes to rest at the edge of my mouth. That swarm of tiny butterflies comes alive again inside my stomach, flittering and fluttering as though caught in a tornado. Even when Mom's voice cracks the stillness of the air and Sam lowers his hand from my face, the butterflies remain strong and loud, bursting with life.

Mom's mouth is moving. Her face is red, and her hands are flailing about. It's a habit. Whenever she talks—or in this case yells—her hands are in constant motion, as though she's putting on a puppet show, but without the actual puppets. But all I can hear is the rush of blood in my ears from the whirlwind in my stomach. My heart is pounding, partly from having to run to the house, partly from the sensation that Sam's fingers are still touching my skin, and partly from the fear of Mom. The combination of all three is overwhelming, and I'm not sure whether to laugh or cry.

"We shouldn't have come up here!" Mom snaps. "I'm calling Peter. We're going home."

She rushes up the stairs and slams the door behind her.

I walk into the guest bedroom. Sam is once again on the lawn mower moving up and down across the backyard. I watch him through the window until he disappears around the north side of the house, the rumble of the engine getting softer and softer. I sit at the edge of the bed and dig my painted toenails into the soft fibers of the pale Berber carpet. Peter will do whatever Mom wants. If she demands we leave, we'll be in first class on the next commercial flight out of Kalispell because she won't want to wait for the private jet. Once home, she'll keep me locked up until the end of August. I'll have surgery, and after the bandages are removed and my skin heals, she'll have me back to work. Her work. Her life. I'm Mom's slave—born to follow in her footsteps, just like she said, and to take shit from her until the day she dies. Or, until the day I die.

From the top of the dresser, the bottle of Extra Strength Tylenol teases me. I could swallow the whole thing right now. Lock the bedroom door, lie back on the bed, and just let those pills put me to sleep. Then what would Mom have? But I can't. Not because I'm afraid, but because if I kill myself, she'll blame it on Peter and Zach, and they'd never forgive me. My eyes sting with tears as the tension rises in my neck and shoulders, and then I'm sobbing like a baby, so hard my breath catches in my lungs. I bring my knees up into my chest, my toes curled, my bottom lip quivering. I'm just like a baby—small and weak and helpless. Clarissa was right about me. I'm spineless.

The bottle of Tylenol calls to me again, but as I stand up to grab it, I realize the steady hum of the lawn mower's engine is gone. Silence. I wipe the tears from my eyes, the snot from my nose, and run into the kitchen. Mom's voice is loud and angry, ricocheting like a racquetball against the walls inside the master bedroom. I imagine Peter holding the phone away from his ear, biting his lip, and sweating like I've seen him do so many times before when she screams. I used to wonder what was going through his head, but I know. I know because the same thing goes through my head. When will she stop? When will she *ever* stop?

Outside the kitchen window, Sam is locking the lawn mower into place on the trailer, the back of his T-shirt wet with sweat. It'll never stop until I make it stop, until Peter makes it stop, and neither of us has the guts to do it.

Time slows to a crawl as Sam pulls his truck keys from the pocket of his jeans. He opens the driver side door and crawls into the cab. He leans over and starts the engine. As the truck backs out of the driveway, my legs tremble. Mom is no longer yelling. I look up as the door to the master bedroom opens. And then I'm running. Out the kitchen door and to the passenger side of Sam's truck, my arms waving, my voice shouting for him to stop and take me with him.

-9-

We're just a few miles south of the house when Sam pulls off the highway and onto a gravel parking area used as a scenic lookout. Several hundred feet below us is Flathead Lake. He kills the engine and turns to me.

"What are you doing?" he asks.

My stomach is upside down, like I'm dangling from a tree by my ankles, and my hands are damp with sweat. I imagine Mom, a few hours from now, frantically searching the house, screaming my name, her life flashing before her eyes as she realizes I'm gone, disappeared. No more auditions. No more shoots. No more dream. And I can't help but feel sorry for her.

I spread my fingers out across my thighs. "I don't know."

"Will she call the police?"

I look at Sam. "Maybe." But I don't actually know what she'll do. I've never done anything like this before.

He sighs. "I should take you back, Melanie."

And he's right. I know he's right. If we turn around now, he can drop me at the top of the driveway, and I can pretend I went for a walk. I don't think Mom would've made it down the stairs and into the kitchen in time to see me get into Sam's truck. But then what? She'll make me pack my stuff, and we'll leave, and I'll never see him again.

"No," I say. "Just let me go with you for a little while." I pull my cell phone from the back pocket of my jeans. "I'll call her and tell her I'll be back soon."

Sam drops his forehead against the steering wheel.

"Please," I say.

Without sitting back up, he turns his head toward me. "Just for a little while."

I nod, then jump out of the truck and walk toward the guardrail. On the other side is a rock cliff—a straight drop to the beach below. I dial Mom's cell number and bite my lower lip.

She answers in half a ring. "Melanie? Where the hell are you?"

"I'm fine, Mom. I—"

"You get back here right now. We're going home. I should've known better than trying to do this with you. Peter said it would be fine, but he thinks he knows everything, and he doesn't, and I do everything for you, and I should've known better...."

I lower the phone from my ear. The lake is a deep green in some places where it's still as glass, and dark blue in others where the wind has created a choppy mess of white caps. In those spots, sailboats glide across the surface, cutting straight through the jagged waves. I always thought the ocean was beautiful, but when I stand on the beach and look out at the horizon, I see nothing but water and sky. Here, there are blue mountains rising from the water's edge like gentle giants. And there are islands too, one big and a few smaller, light brown in color and speckled with trees.

Mom's voice rises to my ears like deadly gas from a canister, crackling and hissing, seeping into my soul and poisoning me.

Stop. Please, stop.

The tension returns to my back and neck, and as it creeps up into my face, my throat begins to burn. Sam is resting his arm on the edge of the window, his sleek black hair glistening in the sun. He's watching me with those dark eyes, but not in the way other boys watch me. He sees *me*. The real me. The person trapped underneath the heavy weight of what's become my life. He doesn't know what I looked like before the accident, and he doesn't seem to care. He smiles, and I stop listening to Mom's voice, like fingernails raking a chalkboard. I smile back, and then push the red END CALL button on my phone. The raking stops.

As I walk back to the truck, Sam says, "All good?"

I smile and nod, then jump into the passenger seat.

"I have another place to take care of a little farther down the road," he says. "You can come with me and hang, and then I'll take you back. Okay?"

"Sure," I say.

He pulls onto the highway. My cell phone vibrates in my hand. Mom is calling. I switch the volume to mute and tuck the phone back into my pocket, my hands shaking. We leave the dark asphalt and white striped lines behind as Sam turns onto a gravel road that skirts the shoreline. At the end of the gravel road is a small summer cottage, its back deck just feet from the water's edge. The rest of the property—a massive swatch of green grass dotted with apricot and plum trees—stretches to the north and west of the cottage. I forget about Mom.

I lean forward and place my hands on the dashboard. "You have to mow all of that?"

Sam smiles. "It looks bigger than it is. Mr. Wetherelt's lot's about the same size, just shaped differently." He opens the door. "Come on. I'll show you the place. Nobody's home."

I follow him onto the front porch of the cottage.

"The Martins gave me a key when I first started working for them." Sam opens the screen door. "They live in Arizona during the winter and spring, so I pretty much take care of it all year. They come up in late July usually and stay through to the first part of October." He pulls a single key from the front pocket of his jeans. "They have two grown sons and a few grandchildren who come and visit in August, but otherwise, it's empty. I stay here a lot. When I can't deal with my dad." He inserts the key into the door handle and pushes the door open.

The place is small—a tiny kitchen, a combined living and dining room, and two bedrooms separated by a bathroom. The floors are made of cherrywood and a stone fireplace is nestled into one corner of the living room. A large rectangular window overlooks the back deck and lake. I was in a place like this once for a commercial, but it wasn't a real house. It was put together in a studio, and at the end of the shoot, the walls were torn down and carted away to make room for the next make-believe location—maybe a seaside bungalow, or a coffee shop in Paris, or a ski chalet high up in the mountains of Vermont. But this isn't pretend. It's a real house on a real lake, and I'm standing in the middle of its living room with a real boy. Sam walks to the window and places his hands on his hips.

"Not the worst place in the world to live," he says. He turns to me. "Can't imagine you have a view like this in Los Angeles."

I shake my head.

"Neither do I, except when I come here." He looks back out the window. "When the Martins are home, I sometimes park on the other side of the highway and hike up the hill to the highest point. Take a sleeping bag. The property belongs to a guy down the road who keeps horses on it in the winter. In the summer, the horses are in the lower pasture, so there's nothing up there but hawks and coyotes. It's quiet. I lie back and watch the stars. Listen to the coyotes and the crickets."

I walk to the window and stand beside him.

"When there's a full moon, I can see the whole lake from up there," he says, "and I feel like I'm the only person left on earth. It's amazing." He smiles. "Never mind the lights along the shoreline."

"Sounds like heaven to me," I say.

"It is. For a little while." He looks at me. "But then I come down off that hill and go home, and I'm as far away from heaven as anyone could be." He turns and walks back into the foyer. "Come on. There's a hammock out front you can rest in while I work."

The front door creaks, but I remain at the window, the lake sparkling like God just poured a million tons of silver glitter on its surface. I can't pull away from the shimmering spectacle, as though I've been hypnotized, and for a second, I think about Mom back at the house and wonder what she must be feeling right now. I think about Peter and Zach, alone and happy and enjoying their long summer days without us. And then I think about Sam, sitting on the top of that hill in the dark, gazing out across a world he wishes were empty except for himself, and I wonder what about his home makes him feel as far from heaven as any person can be.

When he places his hands on my shoulders, I jump.

"It's okay, Melanie," he says. "It's just me."

I don't realize I'm crying until I turn around and Sam pulls me into his chest, my tears soaking into his T-shirt. I inhale the scent of musky deodorant and sweat and cut grass, and I hold it in my lungs until I feel like I'm going to explode. When I exhale, Sam's body folds into mine, and I wrap my arms around his waist. I listen to the steady thumping of his heart, the sound becoming a vibration, an actual tapping from his chest into my ear, and I don't want to let go. Ever.

His arms are around me, warm and tight, strong like steel. He presses his lips to the top of my head, and then gently strokes my hair with one hand. My entire body comes alive, like a string of twinkling holiday lights, and I smile. I don't know what's happening to me, or how it happened. I don't know this boy, but somewhere deep inside of me, I think I do, that maybe we'd been together in another lifetime, hundreds or thousands of years ago before there was anything but water and earth and sky.

I move my face away from Sam's chest and look at the small dimple in his chin, at the tip of his nose, and into his eyes. Strong eyes, but sad. I want to ask him how he knows me, but he places his finger on my lips for a brief second, and when he lowers his hand, he moves his mouth to mine and kisses me. Quiet. Gentle. And even though it is nothing but a small peck, a split second of our mouths touching, I'm standing in the middle of a fire, and for the first time in my life, I am free.

-10-

I'm resting in the hammock tied between a pair of plum trees not far from the front porch of the cottage. The sun is beating down on my face and bare arms, warming my skin. In the air is the hum of the lawn mower and a breeze that caresses the scar on my cheek. I don't know how long Sam and I stood in the small living room wrapped in each other's arms, but when his voice broke the silence to say it was time to get to work, my heart sank a little in my chest. I didn't want to move. I didn't want to go back to Mom.

"Let me get through this, and we'll figure out what to do," Sam had said.

But there's nothing to figure out, really. When he's done, he'll drop me off at the Wetherelt's house, and I'll deal with Mom's wrath, then I'll pack my suitcase, and we'll be gone. There's no way out of this. I look at the small cottage, a little fairy tale torn from the pages of a script. Yes, it's a real place, but it's actually no different than any of the shoot locations I've worked on over the years. At the end of the day, it's gone.

The lawn mower is idling. I sit up in the hammock. Sam has stopped the machine and is talking on his cell phone. I swing my legs over and slip my feet back into my flip-flops. Anxiety ripples through me when I think about Mom, about saying goodbye to

Sam. I place my hand over my stomach to try and steady the rising nausea.

Sam turns the lawn mower around and heads in the direction of his truck, but I know he hasn't finished trimming the entire length of the property, so I walk toward him. His face has changed—his lips are stretched tight and thin and turned down at the corners, and his forehead is furrowed. His eyes have narrowed to small slits across his face. He doesn't look at me as he passes. When he reaches the truck, he drives the lawn mower onto the trailer, shuts it down, and jumps to the ground.

"We have to go, Melanie," he says.

That same sinking feeling swallows my heart. "Why?"

Sam locks the mower into place, his hands working swiftly, his jaw muscles tense. "We just have to go." He climbs into the driver seat of the truck and starts the engine.

No. Not yet. Please.

I remain still until he leans forward to look at me. The anger has washed from his face. His eyes are sad again, and tired. He frowns.

"I don't have time to explain it," he says.

I walk to the truck and climb in, my vision blurred by the tears in my eyes.

"I'll never see you again, Sam," I say.

He puts his hand on my knee. "What do you mean? You talked to her. You said it was all good, right? You're here all summer. I'll drop you off now, and I'll come back another day. If your mom doesn't want you talking to me, we'll figure something out."

"No," I say. "It wasn't all good. I hung up on her."

He leans back in his seat. "Shit."

"We'll be gone by tonight. Tomorrow morning at the latest."

Silence.

I know there's nothing we can do. I can't just run away with him. I don't know where I am. I don't really know Sam.

I don't really know Sam.

My face starts to burn, and then itch. "What is this? Why are you doing this?"

He looks at me, puzzled. "What? What am I doing?"

I reach up, grab the rearview mirror, and take in the raw redness of my scars, the bubbling green of my eyes like foaming algae on a dirty pond.

"I'm hideous, Sam!" I snap. "You can't look at my face and honestly tell me you like what you see. Why are you doing this? Do you feel sorry for me? Is Peter behind this? Did he and Mr. Wetherelt set this up?" My legs are shaking.

Sam puts his hands up in the air. "Melanie, what are you talking about? Who's Peter? I take care of Mr. Wetherelt's yard, and that's it."

I drop my face into my hands and cry. I want to believe him. I want to believe a boy like Sam could fall in love with an ugly girl like me, but it's not possible. No boy I've ever met would look twice at me with these scars on my face unless he was getting paid to do it, getting paid to be nice to me in the months before I get my old face back.

Sam puts a hand on my shoulder. "Melanie. Please look at me."

I sit back and wipe the tears from my eyes.

He leans forward and slides his hand to the back of my neck. "I told you. When I saw you at the edge of the lake, I just...I felt something. I didn't want to feel it, but I did. I can't explain it." He moves back again, places both of his hands on the steering wheel, and stares at his fingers. "I'm a twenty-year-old Indian who still lives on this reservation, mowing people's lawns in the summer and working odd construction jobs in the winter. My father's a drunk. I live in a two-bedroom trailer with him. My mother's been dead for eight years, killed in a drunk-driving accident. She was driving." He looks at me.

"How do I know Mr. Wetherelt's not paying *you* to be nice to *me*?"

The pain in his eyes is deep and heavy, like a black hole. I've never met anyone like Sam, and I'm suddenly scared and embarrassed at the same time.

"I'm sorry," I whisper. "Please don't take me back yet."

His cell phone rings. As he answers the call, I pull my own phone from the back pocket of my jeans. I'd turned it off when we first arrived at the cottage. I hold down the ON button and watch the screen flicker with vibrant colors, and then shine with my wallpaper photo of a daisy. There are twelve missed calls—eight from Mom, four from Kurt, and one from Peter—and five voice mails. A lump rises in my throat.

"Yes, I know," Sam says into his phone. "I'm on my way."

"I can't go back there, Sam," I say, my voice straining against the lump, now like a small stone stuck halfway down my gullet. "Please."

He shifts in his seat. "I have to drive to Polson and get my father at the county courthouse. He got into a fight at a bar on Main Street. It's not even noon yet. When I left this morning, he was asleep. I hid his keys. Obviously, he found them."

"I'll go with you."

Sam looks at me. "You think those marks on your face are ugly?" He lets out a hushed laugh. "Those are nothing, Melanie."

It's just past 12:30 when Sam pulls into the parking lot of the Lake County courthouse in Polson, a town that appears a quarter of the size of Kalispell. We crossed a bridge over the mouth of the Flathead River before entering the small town. Below us, boats were pulling people on water skis and kids were jumping off a dock along the shores of a city park. Their voices and laughter echoed across the water and rose to my open window, as though they were personally greeting me.

"What's so funny?" Sam had asked.

I hadn't even realized I was smiling.

Neither of us is smiling now, though.

"Just sit tight, okay?" he says. "I'll go in and get him. If he's still drunk, he can pass out in the bed of the truck so we don't have to deal with his stench in the cab."

I want to tell Sam it's no problem, that I don't mind the stench, but I don't because in truth, I hate the smell of Mom's breath after she's had a few gin and tonics, and I don't want to think about Mom right now. I'd turned my cell phone back off again before we left the Martin's place. I don't know how many more times she's tried calling, but when a patrol car appears behind Sam's truck, I slide down into my seat. The car slows a bit as it passes, but then continues forward before pulling into an empty parking spot next to another patrol car.

We're at a courthouse, Mel.

Sam opens his door and jumps out. "I'll be right back."

I smile at him and nod, my phone clutched in my hand with my thumb resting against the ON button. But I don't push it. My stomach swirls with the sudden sensation that I'm riding on the teacups at Disneyland. I don't know if any of the five messages are from Peter or Kurt, but I'm too scared to listen to any of them. If either Peter or Kurt did leave a voice mail, Peter's would be telling me to stop upsetting Mom, to please try and keep things peaceful, for him and for me. And Kurt's would be scolding me about the possibility of what my actions could do to my face and, in turn, to my career.

There's one way of getting to Peter without actually calling him. I turn the phone on, and when the daisy appears, I quickly dial Zach's number so I don't have to see how many more calls I've missed. I hold the phone to my ear. It rings once.

What if Peter's with Zach, and he sees it's me?

But before I have a chance to disconnect the call, Zach says, "Mel?"

I stop holding my breath. "Yes. It's me, Zach."

"What's going on? Where are you?"

"Where's Peter?" I ask.

"Uh...he was at work until about an hour ago," Zach replies. "Now he's downstairs pacing back and forth. Joanne's yelling at him. What's going on?"

Two police officers emerge from the courthouse and walk down the front steps. I drop my head a little, but when they reach the base of the cement staircase, they turn away from me and walk in the opposite direction.

"Everything's okay," I say. "Just tell Peter I'm fine."

"Do you want to talk to him?"

"No. I don't...no."

"When he came home he was all stressed out," Zach says. "He told me Joanne wants him to fly to Montana, but he said he can't. He's got a big case going on right now and he can't leave."

"He doesn't need to come up here, Zach," I say. "Everything's fine."

"What did you do?"

I'm not sure how to answer his question. I've always done what I'm supposed to do. Anything that's ever been asked of me, I've done it, even when I haven't wanted to. I haven't ever *done* anything outside of what's been expected. I'm a robot. My life is a mechanical operation—get up, look pretty, go to auditions, work, study with Mrs. Orton, go home, go to bed. Wake up the next day and do it all over again. The car accident was a glitch in the system. A minor setback that has caused a temporary program change until the robot has a chance to be repaired.

I laugh. "What did I do?"

"Come on, Mel," Zach says. "You have to tell me."

Sam appears at the top of the staircase, his arm linked with a man whose head hangs forward. The man's face is hidden behind long gray hair clumped together in thick strands. He's wearing dirty jeans and a white T-shirt covered in dark stains. As they make their way down the staircase, Sam uses both of his hands to help his father maneuver the steps.

"I have to go, Zach," I say.

"No," he replies. "Not until you tell me what's going on."

"Please just tell Peter I'm fine," I say. "I just needed to get away from Mom for a little bit. I'll be back there in a few hours. Tell him to tell her that."

"He called Kurt to go up there since he can't."

"What?"

"He'll be there sometime tonight."

I grit my teeth. "Okay, Zach. I really have to go. I'll call you later tonight after I get back and talk to Mom"

"Sure," he replies. "That's *if* Joanne doesn't tie you to your bed and gag you."

There's no humor in his voice. No snicker or giggle. Not even a quiet rush of air signifying the possibility of a muted laugh.

"Very funny," I say.

"I wasn't trying to be funny."

"Bye, Zach."

Sam and his father reach the bottom of the stairs as I hang up the phone. The man's dark cheeks hang like slabs of dried meat, dimpled and creased from years of heavy drinking, and speckled with salt-and-pepper stubble. His thick eyebrows look like giant caterpillars stuck to his face, and when he looks up at me through bloodshot eyes, they creep upward and curve as though they're about to crawl off and hide in the long, oily locks that hang to his shoulders.

"Melanie," Sam says. "Meet Joe. Joe. Melanie." Sam smiles. "See what I mean. Your scars are beautiful compared to this."

"Who are you?" Joe spits through the open driver's side window, his voice carrying the same accent as Sam's, only much thicker. "And what's that on your face? Look like you been fightin' with those hawks. Like a damn cat, I bet." He lets out a wet, crackling smoker's laugh, and I frown when I think about his lungs—probably all black and charred and scraggly like what's left of a forest after a wildfire.

Sam yanks Joe away from the open window and toward the back of the truck. He opens the tailgate and leans Joe against it, then jumps into the bed and with both hands under Joe's armpits, pulls the man up and back until his entire body is in. Joe sits upright for a second, but then rolls back and sideways until he's curled into a fetal position. Sam jumps back out of the truck, closes the tailgate, and returns to the cab.

"He'll be good back there until I get him home," he says. He turns the key and starts the engine. "I'm sorry about what he said to you."

I peer through the back window at the dirty lump of a man passed out and reeking of stale beer and cigarettes. Even from the short distance between where he stood a moment earlier and where I was, I could smell the sickly odor. It reminded me of the bum who was always slumped on the corner of the street near Kurt's office, holding a crooked piece of cardboard with the words Help and Hungry scribbled on it with a nearly dried-up black marker. I tried to give him a dollar once, but Mom slapped at my hand like I was a dog about to pee on an expensive piece of furniture.

My heart is being squeezed like a lemon in a juicer. "Is he going to be okay?"

Sam looks at me for a long time. "I don't know. I don't ever know."

-11-

More than four hours have passed since I left the house, and as Sam pulls off the highway and onto the Wetherelt's driveway, my tongue becomes a dried-up piece of fruit in my mouth. I swallow at the itch in the back of my throat, wishing more than anything I had a bottle of water.

Sam stops the truck. "Do you want me to wait here?"

I asked that he not take me all the way to the house. I could still possibly get away with telling Mom I'd just gone for a long walk. A very long walk. On the drive from Polson, Sam and I programmed each other's numbers into our phones.

I shake my head. "No. It's okay. I'll be okay." I open the door and slide out of the cab, then shut it again and grip the edge of the open window with both hands. "Just...keep your phone close."

"I will," Sam says. "I promise."

As he pulls onto the highway and turns around to head back in the direction we came, my hands and feet go cold and prickly, like I've just dropped them into a bucket of ice. I remain still until the truck disappears around the bend, and then I turn and begin walking down the driveway, my stomach twisting as I replay in my head each minute from the time I ran out of the Wetherelt's house to now. As I get closer, the prickly sensation in my hands and feet turns into sharp pins and needles as the reality of what I've done settles over me, and I realize I have no idea how Mom is going to react. This is uncharted territory, something I never would've even considered doing before the accident. Before Clarissa showed up with Decker to humiliate me. Before I met Sam.

Sam.

The twisting and writhing in my stomach calms and the butterflies return, more alive than before, fluttering about with the heat that's rising in my body, and for the final few seconds before I reach the front door of the house, there's nothing but warmth and light.

Sam.

But then I open the door, and I'm stepping out of summer and into an icy-cold blizzard. I don't hear Mom's voice at first, but then her screams sting at my ears like a million biting insects, and the sharp pain of her hand slapping my face sends a searing flash of heat throughout my entire body. Before I have a chance to cover my head, she hits me again, and the force of the second blow causes me to lose my balance. I tumble backwards and hit the door before landing on my butt on the ground.

For a brief moment, everything is quiet and still, like the world stopped spinning. I'm not entirely sure if what just happened is real, but then my top lip is wet and when I open my mouth, I taste the salty bitterness of blood on my tongue. It's coming from my nose. I pull my knees up to my chest and wrap my arms around them. Mom hit me. She actually hit me, and hard enough to make my nose bleed. And now she's standing over me, and I'm too terrified to move.

She sighs, deep and heavy like she's been holding her breath for hours and only just now released it. I don't actually feel the air from her lungs, but I smell the familiar mix of sweet and dry that accompanies her gin and tonics. I think maybe that sigh was filled with anguish or regret, but when Mom speaks, I know it wasn't filled with either.

"How dare you treat me this way," she says. She leans forward and points her finger at me. "I've given everything to you, and this is how you thank me? By running off like a little whore with some greasy gardener?"

Even though the pain in my chest is as sharp as though someone just kicked me, I sit still, the blood from my nose now trickling down my neck and soiling my shirt.

"Why are you doing this to me?" Mom asks. "Do you know how much I've sacrificed for you? Do you? It's bad enough you almost destroyed your face in that stupid accident, but now you pull this shit. I just don't get it, Melanie."

She starts walking away from me and into the kitchen, but then stops. "Oh, and it took a little while with the time change, but I got his name from Mr. Wetherelt. I told the police he kidnapped you. They're waiting for him at his house. You won't be seeing him again." She disappears then. "Kurt's coming tonight to take us home, so don't you dare think about leaving this house again." The ice in her glass clinks as she retrieves her drink off the kitchen counter.

I lower my face into my hands, smearing blood across my cheeks. As I rise to my feet, my head spinning, I trace with my trembling fingers the outline of my cell phone in my back pocket. I want to turn and open the front door, run out into the warm air and chase Sam down the highway, but I don't. It's too late. At least fifteen minutes have passed since he dropped me off, and he told me this morning he only lived five miles away. I place both of my hands on the door as tears slip from my eyes.

"What have I done?" I whisper.

Mom walks back out from the kitchen. "Go clean up your face."

I curl my fingers against the door until my nails are scraping at the wood. There's a mild ache in my throat and chest as I turn to face her, but when my eyes meet hers, the ache comes alive, like thousands of tiny animals are trapped inside my body, trying to get out.

"You have something to say to me?" Mom snaps.

I swallow at the digging and clawing in my throat, then take a deep breath and walk past her and into the kitchen. I pull a butcher knife from its protective place in the wooden knife block and turn back around to face her. She stands with one hand on her hip, the other holding her sweating glass.

"What are you doing, Melanie?" she asks. Her eyes shift and her mouth droops subtly as I guess she's now trying to figure out whether I'm threatening her or myself, and then whether or not it's actually just a threat.

"What have you done for me?" I ask.

I hold the knife at my side because I'm not really sure what I'm doing with it. I'm on a movie set, but I'm not "in character." I'm me, standing in front of Mom, anger so alive and boiling up inside of me that I'm afraid I might start spitting flames. I guess this is what happens when you've accepted that your life is not your own, so rather than stand up for yourself, you bite your tongue through its entirety and let people walk all over you. I guess this is what happens when you realize you have nothing, and by having nothing, you have nothing to lose. No friends. No father. Not even a man you can call dad because you're not allowed to. And no mother. No mother.

"You don't give a shit about me," I say. "You never wanted me in the first place. You only gave birth to me so you could blame someone for your ruined life. I never wanted to be you, but you never gave me a choice. And even now, with my face like this, I still don't have a choice because it's not my face, is it? It's your face, Mom."

She sets her glass on the counter and takes a step toward me. "Put that thing down, now."

I lift my hand and point the tip of the knife at her. "What're you gonna do, Mom? You've already taken my life." I turn the knife around and press the blade against my neck. "What difference does it make if I jam this thing in my throat?"

For a brief moment, I forget about Peter and Zach and how Mom would blame them for my suicide, just as she blames me for the car accident that sliced up my face. I think only of the panic in her eyes at the first spurt of blood from my punctured carotid artery—the sheer terror at the sight of *her* life spilling out onto the Wetherelt's tiled kitchen floor. She'd have no clue what to do, and I'd die slowly, all the while witnessing her frenzied attempt to save me…to save *her*.

My cell phone vibrates in my back pocket. I'd switched the ringer off on my walk to the house, just in case Sam called. I didn't want Mom to hear it. I take a step back, the knife still pressed to my throat. Mom doesn't move. Her hands are now shaking, and her eyes are wide and bright like a cornered cat. I reach back and pull my phone from my pocket. Without shifting my gaze from Mom, I hold the phone out so I can check who's calling.

Sam?

"Who is it?" Mom asks, her voice catching with the quick release of air she'd trapped in her lungs.

I lower the knife from my neck. As I walk past her and toward the front door, I turn the blade so it's once again pointed in her direction.

"It's Kurt," I say, as I open the door and step outside.

I wait until I've closed the door before I drop the knife and run in the direction of the highway, my cell phone clutched in my hand. When I'm a good distance from the house, I stop and dial Sam back.

He answers after the first ring. "Melanie?"

"Sam! Sam! I'm so sorry! I'm so sorry!"

"Melanie," he says. "Calm down. What's going on?"

"I don't know, I…wait. Wait. Where are you?"

"I had a bad feeling," he says. "I pulled off the highway just a mile up the road. I wanted to hear from you before I kept going."

"Turn around!" I say. "Turn around and come get me. Hurry, Sam! You can't go home. The police are waiting for you there. Come back and get me!"

"What?"

A surge of magnetic energy—like the hum in the air right after a bolt of lightning flashes across the sky—zips through me, and then I'm running so fast I can barely feel my legs. When I reach the top of the driveway, Sam's truck is in the distance racing toward me. He doesn't stop, but rather slows to a crawl, just enough so I can jump into the passenger seat, and when my door is closed, he slams his foot on the gas pedal.

I don't turn around to see if Mom is running after me. She wouldn't be. She'll figure out soon enough I'm gone, and when the police report back to her that Sam didn't come home, she'll know we're together. And they'll find us eventually, and when they do, I'll have to confront Mom again, and I *will* be on a plane back to Los Angeles. But for now, I just want to be.

-12-

"There's blood all over your face, Melanie," Sam says. He leans forward, opens the glove compartment, and hands me a small stack of paper napkins. "What the hell's going on?"

I wipe at the blood around my nose and on my mouth. "She hit me."

Silence.

"Oh, Melanie. I'm…I'm sorry I wasn't there." He checks his rearview mirror. "I have to ditch this trailer. It'll slow us down too much, and I can't take it up the road to Steve's."

I flip down the sun visor in front of me. Through the tiny square mirror, my scars appear darker beneath the dried blood now caked on them. I dab a napkin on my tongue and wipe the remaining mess away.

"Who's Steve?" I ask.

Sam pulls off the highway and drives down a small dirt road. On one side of the road is a cherry orchard. On the other is a fenced-in pasture overgrown with tall yellow grass.

"My brother," he says. "He's got a place out in the woods. It's our best shot."

Sam stops the truck in front of a closed cattle gate with a sign attached to it that reads NO TRESPASSING. He opens the gate and backs the trailer several hundred yards into the pasture before stopping at the base of a cluster of old pine trees.

"Nobody will find it here," he says as he gets out of the truck again to unhitch the trailer.

Beyond the pasture, on the other side of the road, is the cherry orchard, the branches of its trees just starting to brighten with fruit. And above those rounded trees are hills speckled with pine and fir and scattered shrub. Below it all is the lake, blue and green and white. As I wait for Sam to finish with the trailer, I think about Thomas Kinkade, his paintings alive with every color of the rainbow. Each time I've seen one of his pieces, I've been overwhelmed with a strange longing, like I want to simply step into the artwork and disappear into his magical world and never return. I'd see in those paintings an escape from my life. But this is the first time I've felt that way when looking at something real and touchable, not made of oil and canvas, and that strange longing is so strong now I can actually feel my body being pulled, like there's a giant magnet out there somewhere and my heart is made of iron.

Once on the dirt road again and heading back to the highway, Sam says, "That'll work for now."

The trailer is nearly invisible tucked beneath the overhanging branches of the pine trees. Sitting on that trailer is Sam's livelihood, the means by which he takes care of himself and his father, and in just the short amount of time he's known me, I've changed that. And depending on what happens now and what Mom decides to do, possibly forever.

"Are you sure it'll be there when you come back?" I ask, trying to convince myself Sam will, in fact, return another day to retrieve it and continue on with his life, as though he hadn't met me at all.

"This property belongs to a doctor in Missoula," he replies. "I take care of his yard around the cabin down at the water, but he hasn't done anything with the upper lot. The guy he bought it from used to keep horses on it in the summer, but Dr. Watson doesn't have horses. I guess he doesn't want to pay to maintain it. There's a handful of locals who actually give him money so they can store their boats on the lot in the winter. That's what made me think of dumping the trailer there. If Dr. Watson by chance sees it, he'll think it belongs to one of those locals."

My hands are folded together on my lap, parts of them still caked with dried blood. "I'm sorry for all of this, Sam."

He stops the truck where the dirt road meets the highway. "We'll get this worked out, Melanie. It'll be okay. I'm not worried." He places his right hand over both of mine. "I knew I wasn't supposed to go home. I felt it. Just like I felt something when I saw you at the lake. I had to stop and wait, and when I didn't hear from you, I knew I had to call." He looks through the back window and into the bed of the truck. "Steve's not gonna be happy about this."

I'd forgotten about Joe, still curled into his same fetal position as though the truck hadn't been moving at all. I wonder if he's even still alive, but then he lifts his head for a second, as though startled, before letting it drop back down like it's made of stone.

"Maybe this is a good thing, Melanie," Sam says as he drives onto the highway heading north toward Kalispell. "Steve and Joe haven't talked to each other in years, not since my mother's funeral. Steve was sixteen when she died. He blames Joe. After we buried her, he packed a bag and left and hasn't come back. I drive up and see him two or three times a year, and he welcomes me, as long as I come alone."

I look back at Joe. "Why does he blame him?"

"They were out together the night she died," Sam says. "They got into a fight at the bar. Joe had the keys to the car, but I guess he threw them at her and told her to go home, that he didn't want her there anymore. So, she did. She was wasted. Crossed over the highway into an oncoming eighteen-wheeler."

"Oh, Sam. I'm so sorry," I say. I squeeze my fingers together. "And now this. If you go home, Mom'll make sure you go to jail. This is all bad. I can't do this to you."

Sam laughs. "This isn't bad at all. In fact, it's amazing." He holds his smile. "Do you know how long I've wanted to do this? Show up at Steve's with Joe and just leave him there? Tell Steve it's his fucking turn to take care of Dad for a little while?" He laughs again. "No, Melanie, this isn't bad at all. This is good. Really, really good."

Sam's eyes are wide and bright and fixed on the highway in front of him, but I get the feeling he's seeing something different than just pavement and lines. He smiles again, like we're not sitting in his truck running away from the police at all, but rather in a movie theater watching the most exciting film he's ever seen.

"But what about the police?" I ask. "Won't they be able to trace you to your brother? They'll find us, Sam."

"Even better," he replies, smiling. "They'll take me away and leave Joe there. Steve won't have a choice."

I want him to stop smiling.

"Don't worry," he says. "I'm the only one who knows where Steve is. Joe doesn't even know he's still here. Thinks he left the state altogether. Besides Melanie, nobody's gonna come looking for me. Your mom can scream and shout all she wants. They'll consider this a missing person case, but not for twenty-four hours. And even if you were never heard from again, I could come back and turn myself in and nothing would happen to me. I'm a tribal member. The federal government won't mess with even the most serious crimes on the reservation. At worst, I'd spend a few days in jail."

A strand of Sam's dark hair has pulled loose from the elastic tie at the nape of his neck. It whips across his cheek, up and down as though it's dancing. He turns to me, his lips still clinging to a thin smile, and my heart sags like a waterlogged towel. I think Sam must sense the weight of it because the smile disappears from his face and his eyes narrow and dull.

"What's wrong, Melanie?" he asks.

I want to cry, but I hold my breath instead until some of the water is expelled from my heart and I can actually feel the beat of it again. For the first time in my life, I *want* the movie. I want to be rescued from the wicked witch by a handsome stranger and disappear into the sunset with him while fleeing from a police army. But this isn't a movie. Once Sam delivers Joe to Steve, he can turn right back around and drop me off, and he'll be fine. He can go home. Just like that. No arrest. No prison sentence. He can retrieve his trailer from the lot and go back to work tomorrow and not have to worry about Joe, and I'll leave with Mom and Kurt and return to the misery of my life, only from now on, it'll be worse. There is no happy ending to this with music and credits and an after-party.

"I should've just let you go," I say. "I didn't know what would happen. I only knew Mom called the police. She said I'd never see you again."

"What are you talking about? I'm glad you called me."

"Yeah. You can be free of Joe."

Sam slows the truck, pulls to the side of the road, and shifts the gear to park.

"I don't want to be free of Joe, Melanie," he says. "And I don't want to be free of you. I came back to get you because I knew I had to, and I'm not bringing you back there."

He leans over, takes my face in his hands, and kisses me, long and hard, his tongue warm. Goose bumps blanket my skin, then quickly vanish beneath a thin layer of sweat as every inch of my body begins to burn. Sam wraps one arm around my waist and pulls me onto his lap, knocking his hat off his head, and then his hands are holding my face again, and our mouths keep touching and tasting, neither one of us wanting to pull away. There's an ache deep and low in my stomach—something I've never felt before—and I'm terrified at first because I think maybe I've eaten something bad, and I don't want to throw up all over Sam. Not now. But then I realize it's not nausea, and it's not pain. It's exhilarating, like I'm on a roller coaster in the sky.

When we stop kissing, Sam doesn't move his hands from my skin, my tattered and broken face. He just holds me, our lips inches apart, our breathing heavy. My heart is pounding in my chest, and I can feel his pulse through his fingertips—tap, tap, tap. There's no sound except the air rushing in and out of our lungs, and for a moment, I forget where I am. I'm waiting for the director to shout, "And scene." But it doesn't happen. And all I can do is smile.

-13-

I'm sitting next to Sam, my head resting on his shoulder, when he pulls into the parking lot of a small café in the town of Columbia Falls. At almost three o'clock, there's only one other car in the lot, a rust-covered hatchback with two small dogs curled into little balls and tucked against the back window. They raise their heads to look at us as we get out of the truck, but then lose interest and drop their noses back toward their bellies.

Joe is sitting upright now, his legs crossed in front of him and his hands resting in his lap. He's frowning, his lower lip slightly protruding, and his eyes droopy and bloodshot. When Sam walks around the truck, Joe lifts his head a little, but he doesn't speak. For a moment, it seems he doesn't even recognize his son, but then he smiles and nods. Then, he turns to me. I take a step back, afraid of the words that might come rambling out of his mouth, some rude comment about my face like he'd made earlier at the courthouse. But he doesn't say anything. Instead, he smiles, a big toothy grin. I smile back, but then I wonder if he's going to laugh at me, so I turn away.

"I know you," Joe says.

Sam opens the tailgate and jumps into the back of the truck. "No you don't, Dad. You met her a few hours ago at the courthouse. Remember?" He leans forward and takes Joe's hands. "Come on. Slide to the end. I'll help you out."

They try working together, Sam pulling at his father's thin arms and Joe teetering back and forth as he wiggles himself toward the tailgate. I don't know whether to walk to the edge of the truck and help, and then I don't know whether to laugh or to cry. If Joe were a little boy, I might laugh because it would be typical of a kid to want to slide on his butt while his dad pulls at him, like a game of tug-of-war. But Joe isn't a little boy. He's a grown man, three hours passed out after too many morning cocktails and a bar fight. And Sam is not Joe's father. Sam's the child, wishing he had a different life.

Like me.

I look at the two little dogs in the window and blink back tears.

"No," Joe says. "I do know you."

Sam is gripping one of Joe's arms as the man stumbles toward me. "You were in my dream."

Sam rolls his eyes. "Okay, Dad. That's enough. Let's go in and get some coffee, okay? You're gonna need to sober up a bit before we go any further."

Joe stands firm against Sam's attempt to pull him in the direction of the café's front door. He raises both of his hands toward me like he wants to shake mine, but I hesitate.

"It's okay, Melanie," Sam says.

I extend my fingers to Joe. He takes my hand in both of his, gently as though he's cradling a baby bird. His skin is rough, but his grip is soft, and after a few seconds, I relax and let the warmth of his touch settle over me. His eyes are a smoky gray, and at first I don't want to look at them, but then I can't turn away, like I'm frozen. I see beyond the bloodshot haze of booze and battles and into something deep and sad and lonely, as though I'm seeing right into Joe's very soul.

He releases my fingers and nods, then turns and walks with Sam to the front door of the café. I can't move, like my feet are buried beneath the dirt of the parking lot, and I have to lean forward and place my hands on my knees. I'm not sure if it's because I need to catch my breath, but I take in a huge gulp of air anyway, and I hold it in my lungs for a second before releasing it back into the space in front of me. If it were cold outside, I'd imagine that plume of carbon dioxide would look more like steam from a train than a mere exhalation.

"Melanie? You okay?" Sam asks.

I stand upright and will my feet forward. I smile. "I'm fine."

In the café, Sam and I sit next to each other in a small booth with Joe across from us, his weathered hands wrapped around a steaming coffee cup. He gazes at the dark liquid like there's something floating in it so fascinating he can't pull his eyes away. We order water and roast beef sandwiches with cole slaw and french fries, and we eat in silence. Sam ordered scrambled eggs and bacon for Joe, and he fumbles with his fork as he takes small bites from his plate. When our waitress comes back to remove our dirty dishes, she stares at me, and my heart skips as I wonder whether she's seen my face on the news, if she recognizes me as the California girl who's been kidnapped by a local Indian boy and his father. But then I realize she's looking at my scars because when our eyes meet, her face turns red and she hustles away.

"Why are we here?" Joe asks, his voice stronger now that he's had some coffee and food.

Sam leans forward. "It's a long story, Dad."

Joe smiles. "I love stories." He turns to me. "Would you like to hear one?"

The waitress comes back and sets our check on the table.

"We need to get going, Dad," Sam says as he picks it up.

Joe looks at me, not at my scars like the waitress did, but at my eyes, just as Sam had done when we first met.

"I'd like to hear a story," I say, and I shift in my seat, startled by the words that just spilled from my mouth, as though I hadn't spoken them at all, but rather someone behind me did.

Sam lifts his hat and holds it in the air for a second like he's trying to decide whether to throw it across the café, but then he puts it back on top of his head and smiles. "Make it a quick one." He looks at me. "Dad's a collector of old Native American folklore, Melanie. My great-great-grandfather was a Kootenai shaman, a spiritual leader. Dad says it's in his blood. Used to tell us stories all the time when we were kids. Changed them up a bit now and then to fit whatever situation we were in."

Joe laughs into his nearly empty coffee cup. He takes a final sip, and then sets it on the table.

"This is the story of an Indian boy named Strong Wind who lived with his older brother and mother and father at the edge of a lake," he says. "He was known for his wondrous deeds. He took care of his family well. And, he had the power to make himself invisible."

Sam holds the check out in front of him and studies it, as though he's calculating the numbers in his head.

"Many women wanted to marry Strong Wind because of his righteousness, and it was known he'd marry the first woman who could see him as he came home at night. So, he came up with a clever trick to test whether they were truly genuine in heart and spirit." Joe leans forward. "Every night at sundown, Strong Wind's mother would walk along the shore with any girl who wished to make the trial. His mother could always see him, but nobody else could. As he came home, his mother would ask the girl if she could see her son. And each time, the girl would say yes. When asked with what did he draw his sled, every girl lied and gave a false answer."

Sam lays the check flat on the table and folds his hands together. At first, I think he's impatient with Joe, but then he drops his shoulders a little and lifts his eyes in a way that makes me think he's remembering something good and happy.

"Now," Joe continues as he leans back in the booth, "there was a young girl from a faraway place who came to visit the land where Strong Wind lived. She was very beautiful and gentle and kind, and for these reasons, every other woman was jealous of her and made her do things she didn't want to do. They burned her face with coals from the fire so that her skin would be scarred and disfigured, but the young girl was patient and kept her gentle heart and went about her work."

A tickle rises in the back of my throat, and I reach for my water glass.

"Have you heard this one already?" Joe asks.

I sip through my straw, hoping to wash away the tickle, but the water seems to make it worse instead, and I cough.

"One day," Joe says, "this beautiful girl with her scarred face sought to find love, for it had been absent in her life for far too long. Everybody laughed at her and called her a fool. Why would Strong Wind want a girl like that, they said. But his mother received her kindly, and at twilight, took her along the shore. Soon, Strong Wind came home drawing his sled, though nobody but his mother could see him. When she asked the girl if she could see her son, the girl said no. It was the first time anyone had spoken the truth. Strong Wind then revealed himself to the girl, and when she was asked by his mother with what did he draw his sled, she answered correctly." Joe leans forward again and smiles at me. "She was of genuine heart and spirit."

The tickle in my throat is gone, but now it's like I've swallowed a piece of sand paper, and no matter how much water I drink, I can't get rid of the annoying itch. I set the glass back down. In the little rusty car parked outside, the dogs are still sleeping.

"What happened next?" I ask as Sam places his hand on my knee.

Joe sits back and pushes his coffee cup toward the middle of the table. "Her scars disappeared and she married Strong Wind."

I lift my hand to Sam's cheek and wipe a tear from it, then lean forward and place my mouth on his, my own tears slipping over our joined lips before sliding down and across his neck.

"Changes them up a bit now and then, huh?" I ask.

He laughs.

As Joe rises from his seat, Sam kisses me on the forehead.

"Where we going now?" Joe asks.

-14-

When we leave Columbia Falls, we head north on what Sam calls North Fork Road. But unlike any road I've been on in Los Angeles, this one is exactly what a "road" is supposed to be—two lanes and gravel. We follow the north fork of the Flathead River through the Flathead National Forest. Sam says a fire burned through the area a few years ago, but even with the skeletal remains of the trees left behind, the drive is beautiful—green and blue and empty of any steel structures. As we drive along the river and valley, tall mountains in the distance, I understand why people might feel like they're the only humans left on earth when they come to a place like this. And I understand why Steve would choose such a remote location to hide. Sam said in the winter, this road is impassable.

"Steve has to stock up on supplies before the first snow falls, otherwise he's hunting squirrels and drinking water straight from the river all winter long," he'd said.

Joe is sitting between Sam and me. He hasn't spoken a word since Sam told him where we were going. I've never witnessed the color drain so fast from a person's face before as it did from Joe's when Sam mentioned Steve. And just as quickly, Joe's skin blossomed into a rich shade of apple red as the fear of facing his oldest son again was replaced by the anger at discovering Steve had never left Montana in the first place. But Joe didn't say anything to Sam. I guess he realized without a long explanation that Sam felt he had no choice but to keep Steve's new life a secret.

I wish I could run away from Mom the way Steve ran away from Joe. I guess in a way, that's what I'm doing now, but I know in the end, I'll have to return to her. I won't be able to hide in some remote cabin in the Flathead National Forest. Steve was a year younger than me when he did it, but our lives are so very different. He was strong and brave and fueled by something much deeper—the loss of his mother, a woman Sam said he loved and cherished more than anything in the world. I wouldn't know that feeling, and yet, I make excuses for Mom. Even now as the pain lingers near my nose where she hit me, I question whether I can blame her for her actions. Where I leave room for forgiveness, Steve does not, and I can only think this stems from a loss much greater than anything I've ever felt.

We've been driving for just over an hour when Sam pulls off North Fork Road and onto a smaller dirt road that snakes through a dense pine forest. As we bump along, leaving a cloud of dust trailing behind us, sunlight flickers through the branches of the trees—on and off, on and off—like a little kid is playing with a light switch. The air outside cools as we near the river, and I drop the window down further, the smell of pine and rain-soaked wood and damp earth filling my aching nose. I was in a commercial once where the studio produced a similar odor synthetically, and I remember wishing I could capture some of it in a bottle and take it home with me. I didn't know it actually existed in the real world. I close my eyes and inhale its sweetness, letting my brain soak it into a memory where I hope it will remain forever.

Sam slows the truck to a crawl, and then stops. Through the trees is a small log cabin with an old black Jeep Wrangler parked out front. From the back deck of the cabin is an unobstructed view of the snow-capped peaks of Glacier National Park, the same peaks I saw when Mom and I landed at the airport in Kalispell. I can't tell what's below that view, but I'm guessing the river and valley we just spent the past hour driving alongside.

"This is it," Sam says.

The cabin was left to Steve by Bill Tucker, the owner of the place who hired him at sixteen years old to be its caretaker during the ten months of the year when Bill wasn't there. Bill was eighty-two years old at the time, unmarried with no children. When he died last year, he willed the cabin and the five acres it sits on, including two hundred feet of Flathead River frontage, to Steve.

Joe's hands are folded tightly together in his lap in a failed attempt to prevent them from trembling. Small beads of sweat have popped up along his brow line, and with them, the pungent odor of alcohol.

Sam pulls into the short gravel driveway leading to the cabin. He parks alongside the Jeep and kills the engine. His eyes are wide and anxious as though he's contemplating the idea of turning back around. But then he opens his door and slides out of the truck. I follow, holding my door open for Joe, but he doesn't move, and I can't help but feel that I'm again in the presence of a small child, only this time he's not giggly about gliding on his butt across the bed of the truck. Now, his shoulders are sagging and his head is down, like he's about to be punished for being naughty.

"Come on, Dad," Sam says as he walks up beside me.

From the other side of the Jeep comes the sound of a screen door opening.

"Little brother? Where are you?" Steve's voice is deeper than Sam's, but his accent is as thick as Joe's. Heavy footsteps plod across wooden planks, and then crunch on gravel as Steve walks in our direction. "I'm glad you called before you left C Falls. I was about to…."

He stops behind the Jeep, and at first I think he's confused by who Joe is, but then he puts his hands on his hips and says, "What the hell is he doing here?"

Steve is a spitting image of Sam—same long dark hair, same deep brown eyes. The only differences are Steve is a few inches shorter and at least ten pounds heavier than Sam, and rather than just four years older, the premature lines on his forehead and around his mouth give him the appearance of a man in his late forties.

"I'm sorry, Steve," Sam says. "I had no—"

"Damn it, Sam," Steve interrupts. His eyes pass over me quickly before he turns back to Sam. "I told you not to bring him here. Ever. He's not allowed." Steve walks toward Joe, stopping just inches from him, but Joe doesn't look up from the ground. "You're not welcome here. You hear me. You're *not* welcome here!" Steve turns and walks back toward the cabin.

"Wait here with him, will you?" Sam asks me.

"Sure," I reply.

He chases after his brother and disappears inside the cabin. I don't know what to say or do. Joe is silent, staring at the gravel beneath his feet the same way he did into his coffee cup back at the café, but his whole body is now hunched over like a defeated dog. The trembling that started in his hands seems to have moved into his arms and legs, and although the temperature outside must be at least in the sixties, I wonder if he's cold. But then I think maybe it's from a delayed hangover, although it's not likely considering how much Joe drinks, because I've seen Mom's body shake like this after a night of partying too much.

"Do you want to sit back in the truck?" I ask, my voice too sharp and loud for where we are.

As though someone turned on a giant fan in the sky, a sudden wind blows across the property causing the branches in the pine trees surrounding us to sway heavily up and down in an odd sort of dance. Somewhere in the distance, a hawk or an eagle cries, and Joe looks up into the sky as though he's expecting the bird to be right above us.

"Did you know in some native cultures," he says, "the eagle represents spiritual protection? It brings strength, courage, wisdom, and healing."

He points to something above the cabin but far off in the distance, too far away to identify exactly what it is. The object moves back and forth across a sky turning red with the coming dusk.

"No," I reply. "I didn't know that."

"The eagle has an ability to see hidden spiritual truths, rising above the material to see the spiritual. It has the ability to see the overall pattern, and the connection to spirit guides and teachers. The eagle represents great power and balance, dignity with grace, a connection with higher truths."

I shift my focus from the sky to Joe, for just a split second, but when I look back up to where the object had been, it's no longer there. It's now perched on the roof of the cabin—a bird the size of a small child, its caramel and dark chocolate feathers shimmering in the light of the setting sun.

I gasp and take a step back until I'm standing behind Joe.

"It's a golden," he says, and he nods at it as though he and the bird are communicating in some bizarre secret language.

I remember going to the zoo a few years ago in Los Angeles with Peter and Zach. Mom was sick that day, and so she had no reason to keep me at home. In fact, she wanted me to go so I wouldn't catch what she had and be forced out of auditions. A section of the zoo had been set up as a bird sanctuary—a temporary home for smaller hawks and falcons. But there'd been a golden eagle there too, in a separate cage because its wing was broken and it had become too aggressive toward the other birds. The zookeeper told us it would never be returned to the wild because it would never fly again.

"So, it'll spend the rest of its life in this cage?" I'd asked.

"Unfortunately, yes," the zookeeper replied.

While Peter and Zach breezed through the bird sanctuary, I stopped in front of the golden eagle's cage. Something about that bird reminded me of myself—imprisoned and broken and never to be free, never to be released into the world it so desperately wanted to be a part of.

Joe lifts one hand into the air, and as he lowers it again, the eagle opens its mighty wings and flies away, back in the direction it came from. There's a wooshing sound with the rising and falling of its wings, and then the wind blowing through the trees again, stronger now like a storm is coming, but there's not a cloud in the sky. Then, the screen door slams shut, and Sam is walking toward us.

"He agreed to let us stay overnight," he says. "I told him everything. The cabin has two bedrooms. Dad, you can have the guest room." Sam looks at me. "We can sleep on the floor in the living room. Steve has a couple of sleeping bags. I agreed to help him make a run for supplies early tomorrow, but he wants us gone as soon as we get back."

I think about Mom, about Kurt flying to Kalispell tonight, about what they'll both do when they see me, and a knot forms in my stomach, so tight I find myself leaning over in order to alleviate the pain.

"What does that mean?" I ask. "What'll we do then? Where will we go?"

Even as I'm asking Sam these questions, I know the answers. I've known the answers since I jumped into his truck back at the Wetherelt's. When all is said and done, this will be over, and unlike the golden eagle that has now disappeared into an increasingly darkening sky, I will be the one back in Los Angeles, forever destined to look at the world from inside a cage.

"We'll figure it out, Melanie," Sam says. "For now, let's just get some rest. Okay?"

He takes my hand and we walk to the cabin, Joe following several feet behind us. I resist the urge to reach back and put my arm around him, like somehow by embracing him I can offer protection against whatever might happen inside. And from what I just witnessed of Steve, it won't be good. But when we step through the door, Steve is nowhere in sight. The interior of the cabin is one big room that includes the kitchen, dining room, and living room. There are two doors opposite one another, each leading into a bedroom, and a third door—the bathroom, combination laundry room—at the far end of the kitchen. One of the bedroom doors is closed.

I sit down in the sofa across from a large stone fireplace while Sam shows Joe to the second bedroom. They're talking, but I can't make out any of their words. The air in the cabin is cool and smells of wood smoke. On the kitchen counter next to the sink is a dish rack full of clean plates and pots and utensils. Dangling above the sink is a strip of flypaper, speckled with black dots, some of them still moving as they try desperately to pull their hairy feet from the glue. I laugh because Mom once made us wait outside of a building in Santa Monica where auditions were being held because she saw flypaper hanging next to a window. She was convinced I'd catch a disease if I sat in that room for too long.

Staring at the flypaper now, I have the urge to go over and touch it. But instead, I stand up and walk to the sliding glass door that opens onto the back deck. The entire east wall of the cabin is glass, and I understand why. The view is like a photograph in a magazine—a golden valley dotted with trees split in half by a crystal blue river that twists and turns to an unknown destination on the horizon. From that destination, jagged mountains rise sharply toward a mix of reds and yellows and oranges like a Big Stick Popsicle has melted across the sky.

A door opens, and I turn around to face Steve. He walks over to me and shakes my hand. His eyes fall over my scars for a second, but then he looks up and smiles. "I'm sorry I didn't properly introduce myself outside."

"It's okay," I say. "And I'm really sorry about all of this. I didn't mean to be—"

"Don't worry about it," Steve interrupts. He releases my hand. "Just some unresolved family stuff. It's been tough. I'm just not ready to face it. To face him."

Sam emerges from the second bedroom. "You're gonna have to someday, brother. Why not now? He's here, and this won't happen again. You know that."

"I didn't ask you to come here, Sam. And I can ask you to leave. Don't push it."

I step away from Steve, the heat radiating from his reddening face practically warming my skin.

Sam approaches us. "But why can't you two just hash this out? You think this has been easy for me? You think I wanna live like this?"

"You could've left too, little brother," Steve says. "You chose to stay. That's your problem."

Sam yanks his baseball hat from his head and throws it onto the ground. "It's not my fucking problem! It's our problem. He's *our* father, and you know damn well Mom wouldn't have wanted it to be like this. You know that! Why can't you just forgive him?"

Steve pushes Sam in the chest. His legs hit the side of the sofa, and he falls backwards onto the wood floor.

"He killed her," Steve shouts. "He gave her the keys to the car, and he sent her out on that road. He fucking killed her!"

Joe steps into the living room, his face wet with tears. "Please. Please stop."

Steve runs his hands through his hair.

"Fuck this," he says. He walks into the kitchen and grabs his keys from the table, then storms out the front door.

Sam and Joe and I remain still as the Jeep gasps and then roars to life. Tires spin on gravel, the engine chokes, and then there's nothing but a heavy silence and the growing darkness as the last of the day's light slips away.

-15-

Two hours pass before Sam decides to rummage through Steve's refrigerator in hopes of finding something to make for dinner. None of us said much after Steve left. Joe apologized to Sam. Sam told him not to. I stood there as the two men tried to find the appropriate words, and then I realized they'd already said everything they could say to each other in the years since Sam's mother's death. It was Steve and Joe who needed to talk now, but clearly that wasn't going to happen. I thought about Mom, how I've never talked to her, how I can't talk to her, and I felt a sharp stabbing in my chest when it hit me that maybe I'd never be able to. Ever. Joe had turned around then and walked back into the guest bedroom.

We each took a shower, all three of us sharing the one clean towel Sam found in the hall closet. Sam let me go first. The shower was small, but the water pressure strong and the temperature hot. I stood under the shower head for what felt like an hour letting the stream run down my neck and back and legs, taking with it to the drain the sweat and blood from the day.

Mom hit me. She actually hit me.

I washed my hair, using my fingers to comb through it. From a pile of clean laundry on Steve's bed, Sam found sweatpants and

T-shirts for all of us to wear until our clothes were finished being washed and dried.

Sam pulls a pack of frozen veggies from the freezer. In the pantry, he finds an unopened bag of spaghetti and a jar of marinara sauce. I prepare the pasta while he empties the sauce and vegetables into a pan. While we eat, Joe's fingers shake. In the refrigerator, he finds a can of Pabst Blue Ribbon, but Sam grabs it away from him when he turns around with it gripped in his hand. Joe's lower lip quivers and his mouth forms into a thin, tight line. I know he wants to snap at Sam, but he doesn't. If I weren't sitting here, I think he would. He walks to the table and takes his plate, then returns to the kitchen where he rinses it off before placing it in the dish rack. Without looking at us, he walks back into the guest bedroom and closes the door.

Sam puts the beer back into the refrigerator. We clear our plates and put everything away, and while he builds a fire, I push the coffee table to the side and lay the two sleeping bags Steve gave us across the rug on the floor. The budding fire spits and crackles, then kicks to life. Sam fans it one more time before sitting next to me on the sofa. Shadows and light dance across his face, his eyes appearing black in the sharp darkness of the living room.

"I don't know what I was thinking," he says. "I've been waiting for a reason to bring Joe up here. Hoping, I guess, that if Steve actually got to see him, he'd maybe forgive him. My father's aged about thirty years in just eight. Doesn't even remotely look like the person he was before my mother died."

My heart sinks a little. I don't want to just be a reason, an excuse for taking a leap of faith. And since that leap failed, what happens now? Where do we go from here? I turn to the fire, its long dancing tendrils reaching up through the chimney's throat as though some terrified creature is trying to break free from the red fury.

"She was the love of his life," Sam says. "They were high school sweethearts. Started dating their sophomore year. Got married the summer after they graduated and had my brother eighteen months later, then me four years after that. They had their fair share of fights, Melanie, but there was always love. Always lots of love."

Tears fill his eyes. They shake and wobble until he blinks, sending them racing down his cheeks like raindrops on a windshield. I place my hands on his face, but I don't wipe the tears away. Instead, I let them slide over and pool in the spaces between my fingers. He covers both of my hands with his, and for a long time we just sit in silence, listening to the hiss and snap of the fire. When he finally pulls my hands down and moves closer to me, I close my eyes and suck a deep breath through my nose. His fingers are touching my face again, rising and falling with each tiny bump and groove as he gently traces over my scars, as though he's finger painting onto a delicate piece of rice paper.

"Does it hurt?" he asks.

I open my eyes to his—dark and sad and longing for something. Me, I hope, but I'm not really sure. Maybe he just wants answers, like I do.

"No," I reply, but with the slight drop of his head and the tight smile that forms on his lips, I know he's not asking if it physically hurts.

"I don't know," I say. "I think I don't care about what I look like, but then my whole life is my face. I'm scared. I don't really want the surgery because I don't want my life anymore, but I also don't know what else to do."

"You can do whatever you want, Melanie," Sam says. "Surgery or not. And if you go through with it, it doesn't mean you have to go back."

I turn and face the fire again. "I wish I were strong enough to make that decision."

"I think you'd surprise yourself."

I wish I believed Sam, but I don't. I've never been strong enough to do anything.

"You're here," he says.

Yes. I'm here.

I look at him and smile. "I've never done anything like this, Sam."

"You see. You've already surprised yourself."

"Yeah, I guess I did," I reply. I shake my head. "But it's not forever. I try to imagine the future, but all I see is Mom and the surgery, and after that, the same spinning wheel I've been on my whole life. I'll never be free until she's dead, and by then, I'll have been living her life for so long there'll be nothing left for me."

"So...where am I in all of this?" Sam asks.

I swallow at the pain that's now settled in my throat.

"It's okay," he says. "I understand."

He puts one hand on my cheek and holds it there briefly, then moves it back and behind my neck. I close my eyes and let my head fall into his palm, and then the fingers on his other hand are touching my lips. He slides that hand down my neck until it's resting just above my breasts, and then his mouth is pressed against my throat. Both of his hands are in my hair now, gently pulling as he kisses my neck, then under my chin, and then his lips are on mine and our mouths are once again in some kind of deep exploration. That unfamiliar ache returns to my belly, but it's lower now, and more of a pulse than an ache, like a gentle heartbeat. As Sam moves his hand across my breast and down to my hip, the pulse grows stronger and falls deeper until it settles in a place only I've touched.

Sam rises from the sofa and unzips the two sleeping bags, laying one flat on top of the other, and then he helps me to my feet and out of my clothes. We stand naked in front of each other, our eyes dancing in the flickering firelight. He takes both of my hands in his, and I think I'm the only one shaking, but then his fingers are trembling against mine.

"I've...never...."

"Me neither," I say, and I smile.

"I want to, Melanie. I really want to, but I don't have anything—"

I put my fingers to his lips, and then step toward him until my body is pressed to his, the heat of his skin curling around me like a blanket. His chest is smooth and strong. I wrap my arms around his neck and kiss him, and together, we drop down until I'm lying on my back. He covers us with the second sleeping bag, and for the next hour, we seek out and explore those private places where nobody else has been, uncovering little secrets never before shared, but saving the best kept one for another time, another place. When we're both too exhausted to move any longer, I fold myself into Sam, my back against his damp chest, his arms holding me, and I embrace the combination of our rapidly beating hearts, like a tune I've never heard before. And even after I fall asleep, I still hear that beautiful music.

A door slams, followed by a loud bang, and then, "Shit!"

Sam and I both sit up. The living room is pitch black except for a sliver of orange in the fireplace from the dying embers. I grab the edge of the sleeping bag and cover my naked skin as Sam lies on his back and wiggles into his jeans. When he stands up, laughter erupts from the kitchen.

"Sorry, little brother," Steve says. "Can't see a damn thing in here."

Sam steps around the sofa and disappears into the darkness. Several seconds pass before dull light spills into the living room from the small bulb above the kitchen sink. The feet of a chair scrape across the wood floor and I hear the sound of Steve slumping into that chair.

"What time is it?" Sam asks.

"Not a clue," Steve replies, and I realize now he's been drinking.

"Are you drunk?" Sam asks.

"Oh. Probably."

"I didn't think you did that."

Steve laughs. "Drink? Please, little brother."

"No," Sam says. "Get drunk...and then drive home."

"Sorry to disappoint you."

More scraping as another chair is pulled out from under the kitchen table, this one sounding more like a piece of metal being dragged across concrete, and I pull the sleeping bag up to my chin as a chill runs up the length of my spine.

"I'm just surprised is all," Sam says. "Seems it'd be the last thing you'd do, considering."

"Why don't you just mind your own goddamned business," Steve says. "What the fuck you care anyway?"

Silence.

Steve sighs. "Sorry, Sam. I didn't mean that."

More silence.

"Thing is," Steve says, "it's not always easy being up here alone. You call me this afternoon and tell me you're coming up and you got a girl with you, and I was so damn happy for you, Sam. And then I see Joe with you, and I want to keep being happy for you, but I'm so pissed. I'm so pissed because I don't want to hate him, but I do. And I do so much it sometimes feels like it's just eating me alive. All this hate and anger. Mom was never like that, you know."

"No," Sam says. "She wasn't."

"And neither was Dad. But here I am, and it's because of them. Both of them that I'm out here, alone and mad, feeling like I can't go anywhere or do anything. Like I'm trapped. And I just don't want to be trapped like this anymore."

Tears bite at my eyes. I pull the sleeping bag over my face and inhale the smell of wood smoke and pine sap and bug spray, all mashed together and stuck in the wool fibers in a way that will keep them there forever.

"You don't have to be trapped like this," Sam says. "Just talk to him. Hear what he has to say. We lost Mom, Steve, but he lost his best friend. His soul mate. You remember when we were kids and he told us the story about how his elders came to him in a dream and showed him Mom? That's how he knew they were supposed to be together? They were united in spirit."

Steve laughs. "I can't believe you remember all his crazy stories."

"I'm not sure they're all so crazy," Sam says. "Dad knows things. He feels things, and I'm starting to feel things too, and I wonder if it's not something in our blood. Something passed down from our ancestors like he says."

Silence again.

Sam lowers his voice, but I hear his words. "When I saw Melanie standing there at the water at Gordon Wetherelt's place, I had to look twice because I swear to you on my life, I saw Mom.

And then when she turned around and I realized it wasn't Mom, there was this feeling in my chest, like the air was being sucked out of me, and I just knew somehow that I was supposed to meet her. And that maybe she was supposed to meet me. That we were meant to help each other in some way, but now I think I'm just in love with her, and maybe that's what it is. I fell in love with her at first sight, like Dad fell in love with Mom." He laughs. "But that's crazy. Isn't it?"

Steve clears his throat. "I don't…know, little brother."

He's in love with me.

My body is buzzing beneath the sleeping bag. I want to throw it off and run into the kitchen, wrap my arms around Sam and tell him I love him too, because I do, deep inside my heart in a space that's warm and alive and happy. I felt something too when I met him—an undeniable twinge of what I thought was recognition, a fleeting moment of déjà vu. But it wasn't that at all. It was love.

"I need to sleep," Steve says. He groans as he rises from his chair. "You're getting up with me in the morning, right?"

"As long as you have some coffee brewing," Sam replies.

Steve crosses the living room, moving toward his bedroom, his feet dragging across the floor like he's pulling a heavy bag of rocks behind him. "Coffee. Yes."

"Goodnight," Sam says.

"Sam?"

"Yeah."

"Her face," Steve says. "It was a car accident, right? That's why she's here? In Montana?"

"Right," Sam replies. "How'd you know that?"

"I don't know. I just do."

-16-

I wake up to intense light and heat and the smell of coffee and bacon and charred wood from the fireplace. With no blinds on the window, the morning sunshine spilling in has warmed the room up like an oven, and I'm the one being cooked. I reach up and grab my clothes off the sofa, then dress under the cover of the sleeping bag before standing up. Joe is sitting at the kitchen table, one hand gripping the handle of a coffee mug, the other flipping through the pages of a magazine.

"Good morning," I say.

He closes the magazine and smiles. "Yes. It is."

I know my face is turning red, so I grab the sleeping bags and zip them back up, then fold them and place them on the sofa. I don't know how long Joe's been up, but I'm embarrassed by the possibility he might've recognized what took place between Sam and me during the night.

"I made breakfast," Joe says. "I put some in the oven for you."

"Thank you."

I walk into the kitchen and open the oven door to a full plate of scrambled eggs and four slices of bacon. I grab the plate, a clean fork from the dish rack, and a paper napkin, and sit across from Joe.

"Do you want coffee?" he asks.

"No, thanks," I reply. "I've never been much of a coffee drinker. Mom's kept it away from me. Said it would stunt my growth."

He laughs. "So that's why you're so tall. Never drink coffee."

I smile as I take a bite of my eggs.

"Guess that's why I'm so short, huh?" Joe says. "Sally was tall. My wife. Not as tall as you, but I think she was five feet and seven inches. Sam got his height from her. Steve's shorter, like me." He looks down and taps his hand on the magazine. *Sports Illustrated.*

I eat a slice of bacon.

"I'm sorry you had to see all that last night," Joe says.

"It's okay," I reply, before wiping my mouth with the paper napkin. "I'm sorry he's so angry with you."

"I deserve it."

I eat another slice of bacon. I'd like to argue with Joe, but I can't. Just as I can't argue with Mom about why she blames me for the outcome of her life. Once you start blaming somebody for something, it's pretty difficult to break. Everybody but Mom is responsible for where she is, what she doesn't have. Me. My biological father. Peter. Steve will never accept that his mother made her own decision to walk out of that bar and drive home. Just as Mom will never accept she made the decision to have me, even after my father turned his back on her. I have no idea why she did it. Was she trying to get back at him for leaving? Did she think by having me he'd have no choice but to love and support her? He didn't want me just as much as she didn't, so when everything failed and her career took a nose dive, what choice did she have but to blame me? And what better way to get back at me than to force me to live my life for her?

"It's not your fault," I say.

Joe smiles. "I know what you're thinking. She didn't have to drive. She could've stayed at that bar. Maybe she could've gotten a ride home."

I set my fork down on my plate, hoping the memory of last night with Sam will somehow find a hiding place within the folds of my brain.

"Don't worry," Joe says. "I can't read minds."

My face is hot again. I push my plate to the side and lean back in my chair. I'm not relieved by his words. There's something cosmic about him—and about Sam and Steve, although I feel Joe has a better grasp of it than his sons. Joe may not be able to read minds, but he knows things and feels things, just as Sam suggested to Steve last night. And sitting here with him now, I wonder where this conversation is going.

"It's just common sense to think it was as much Sally's fault as mine," Joe says. "She made the decision to get into that car and drive. But she couldn't have done it without the key I gave her."

"But Steve doesn't see it that way," I say.

"No," Joe replies. "He doesn't. When he left a few days after Sally's funeral, I thought he'd come back after a couple of months, once he'd had some time to process everything. I'd talk to him then. But when he didn't return, it was worse than losing Sally."

I sit up again, the smell of cold bacon grease suddenly so thick I can actually taste the bitterness of it on my tongue, like I've just eaten a spoonful. "I don't understand. Sally is dead. How can Steve running away be worse than that?"

"Because," Joe says as he leans forward, "my son lives with anger and resentment and fear, and as a father, that's worse than losing Sally. She's gone to the spirit world where there is no anger or resentment or fear. I count the days until I'm with her again because I know she's forgiven me. She doesn't blame me, but I can't join her until I make things right with Steve."

I think about my conversation with Sam at the Martin's cabin. Joe's a drunk, and Sam's given up the past eight years of his own life taking care of him, and all this time, Joe's only concern is Steve? Joe's been drowning himself in his sorrow of not being allowed to see his wife again because Steve disappeared, and Sam's the one who's had to deal with all of it—his mother's death, his father's self-pity, and his brother's pure selfishness.

My hands are damp with sweat. "What about Sam?"

"Sam knows what's going on," Joe says. "He's always known. He's just not been able to truly understand it. Until now."

"What's there to understand? He's the one who's been the outcast in all of this. Taking care of you, hiding Steve's secret. *And* having to deal with his mother's death this whole time. Alone."

"Oh, but you're wrong, Melanie," Joe says. "Steve tried to take Sam with him when he left. I overheard the conversation. But Sam refused. He wasn't convinced. Much like Sally, he made his own decision. Ask him, and he'll tell you. He knew something was coming. Something that would make him stronger, that would help him understand. He just had to be patient and wait."

"But…."

Joe smiles. "Sound familiar?"

My scars itch, like someone's tickling them with a feather. I reach up and touch the one on my forehead, then on my cheek, as though I need to reconfirm they're still there. And I'm happy they are. They're hideous, but they're mine, and I know if it hadn't been for them, I wouldn't be here. I wouldn't have met Sam.

"I wanted this to happen," I say. "But at the time, I wasn't completely sure why."

"Because you want to be stronger," Joe replies. "You want to understand."

I nod. "Yes."

"There's not always a clear explanation right away when things happen," he says. "Sometimes it takes longer. Days or weeks or months. Even years."

I place my hands flat on the table. "I've been waiting my whole life for a chance to be free, and I thought the accident was it. But then Mom brought me up here, and I sort of decided at that point, I guess, that the only way out would be to kill myself. And then I met Sam."

"You were waiting for each other. Just not in the way one would think. It's more of a feeling or a dream."

I smile. "Yeah. That's right."

Joe stands up, his coffee mug in his hand. "I think I need a refill." He picks up my plate. "Let me take this for you."

My fingers look small and pale all spread out on the table. I'd never really noticed their shape before—long and thin. My nails are trimmed short and bare. They're Mom's hands.

Mom.

I take in a shaky breath, hoping it might ease the pain that's crept into my chest, but it doesn't. I'm sad for Mom. So sad all of a sudden that all I want to do is get away. I walk through the living room and out onto the back deck. The sun has risen above the distant mountains and is now hovering midpoint in the sky—an explosion of shimmering, hot white light. In the valley below, the river glitters, as though beneath its surface are thousands of children holding fourth of July sparklers above their heads. They bounce and twirl and spin with the rapidly moving water.

I wish Mom could see this, and not just see it, but also appreciate it. But I know she wouldn't. I used to believe she wasn't capable, but now I'm not so sure. I think she just needs to believe there's something for her beyond me. She needs to let go of all the anger and resentment and fear. Just like Steve. By doing that, she'd be free. And so would I.

But I also know this can't just take place on its own. She won't simply wake up one morning with a new outlook on life. Something has to happen. Just like my accident, my face, meeting Sam. Maybe there's a plan for Mom too, and by coming here, it's been set in motion—me leaving with Sam yesterday, her slapping me, and now, I'm gone and she has no idea where I am or for how long I'll be away. Is it possible she could be sitting at the Wetherelt's house right now, accepting the notion of change and be willing to talk about it? I guess anything's possible.

I turn around. Sam is walking through the living room and toward me. He steps out onto the deck.

"What are you doing out here?" he asks as he hugs me.

"I had a nice breakfast with Joe," I reply.

He kisses the top of my head. "Did you? Well, I had a nice breakfast with my brother too."

I wrap my arms around his waist and rest my head on his chest. "So, what happens now?"

"It'll be good," Sam replies. "Really, really good."

In the kitchen, Steve is standing across from Joe. They're talking. Joe smiles. And then the two men embrace. Seconds pass, then minutes, but they don't let go. And all the while I'm watching them, I'm floating, suspended above all of the pain and fear. In their moment of understanding, there's something inside of me, pulling and tugging, trying to get out of that trapped place, and for the first time in my life, I feel it releasing.

"I need to go back," I say.

Sam kisses the top of my head again. "I know."

-17-

We spend the rest of the morning sitting on the back deck while Sam and Steve and Joe reminisce about the past. Both boys went to school in Polson. Sam graduated from the high school there. Steve dropped out altogether after Sally died.

"I'm gonna get my GED when I have a chance, though," he'd said. "I'd like to go to Chicago someday. Go to a Bulls game."

They both played basketball in school, but Sam agreed Steve had always been the better player.

"After he left, there was this expectation," Sam said. "I was Steve Burke's little brother. I *had* to be good. But I could never fill his shoes."

"I was short," Steve said. "But I was fast. Got it from Mom."

"She was on the track team in high school," Joe said. "I'd been following her around for a long time. Fell in love with her at first sight. I decided to join the team, but I could never catch her. I could throw a discus better than anybody though. With her legs and my arms, we were a perfect match." He laughed.

Sally was the oldest of three, the daughter of an alcoholic mother who later left and never returned, and a father who was rarely home. He was a good father when he was there, but his absence left Sally in charge of everything. She practically raised her siblings. After she and Joe married, her brother and sister lived with them for several years. Sam was just a baby when the youngest sibling, Reuben, graduated from high school and left the reservation.

"They couldn't wait to leave here," Joe said. "Reuben got as far as Billings. He works for the city. But Sheila stopped in Missoula. She was a dancer."

"She was a stripper," Steve said.

Sam sighed and turned to me. "Sheila got into drugs. She killed herself when she was twenty-seven. That's when Mom started drinking. She blamed herself."

Joe leaned forward then and dropped his face into his hands, and for a long time we let him weep while we remained silent. Every once in awhile, he'd try to control the crying by taking a deep breath, but each time he did, his exhales would come back out in shudders as sobs wracked his body. Steve placed a hand on Joe's shoulder while using the other to wipe the tears from his own cheeks.

I didn't know what images were flashing through Joe's mind at that time, but I wondered if they were of Sally running along their high school track, or of her face when she held each of her newborn sons in her arms, or of the anguish in her eyes when she lost her younger sister. But when Joe lifted his head finally and smiled, I could only think he was seeing her at that moment, reaching out to him in the loving and caring way she always had, and finally welcoming him to join her wherever she was now.

For lunch, Joe and Steve grill bison burgers and corn on the cob. They sit across from Sam and me and ask questions about Mom and Peter and Zach. I say very little. I don't want to share much about my life. Not yet. I want to talk to Mom first before I say anything about her because I want to believe she can change. I want her to be waiting for me. I want her to talk to me, and I want to give her a hug.

Sam rises from his chair and steps behind me, placing his hands on my shoulders.

"You need to go," Joe says.

I stand up. "Yes."

"I understand."

Steve and Joe walk us to the front door. I hug them both and promise to see them soon.

"Oh, you will," Joe says as he squeezes my hands in his.

I look into his eyes, and I'm again feeling as though I'm seeing right into his soul, only this time, there's no sadness. No loneliness. This time there's light and warmth, deep down inside, but when I turn away from him, expecting to feel happy and good, I think I've been punched in the gut instead, like I just walked into something sticking up from the ground in front of me. I stop, as though I *have* actually hit something. Sam is walking forward still, but he turns around and frowns.

"Melanie," he says. "You okay?"

I glance back at the front door of the cabin, but Steve and Joe are already inside.

I put my hands on my stomach and close my eyes. When the feeling passes, I look at Sam. "I'm fine."

"Are you sure you're okay?" he asks as we pull out of the driveway. "We can stay here, Melanie. You don't have to go back."

But he's wrong. I do have to go back. I have to face Mom. And maybe it's the fear of doing it that makes me feel like I'm stuck on a small ship out on rough seas.

"Was your mom like Joe?" I ask.

Sam smiles. "In what way?" He glances in both directions before pulling onto North Fork Road.

"Did she…know things?"

"No," he replies. "At least I don't think so. In fact, she used to mock Joe sometimes. Called him crazy more than once. She'd tell him to quit talking to animals." He smiles. "But Joe introduced her to a lot of things she wasn't aware of before she met him. I mean, she spent her whole life on the reservation, but she didn't know her history. Her culture. By the time I was born, she was a pretty active member. Helped with the yearly powwows and other ceremonies. She even used to volunteer at the cultural center in Pablo once in a while." Sam shifts in his seat. "It wasn't Joe who introduced her to alcohol, though. Just the opposite. And Steve knows it. But Joe couldn't stop her, and every time he tried, she'd get angry. So instead, he joined her."

He couldn't stop her, so he joined her.

"Maybe he was just sad," I say.

Sam reaches across the seat and wraps his fingers around my forearm. He pulls gently, and I scoot over until my leg is pressed against his. I rest my head on his shoulder, and he kisses the top of it.

"And he's not crazy," I say.

"No," Sam replies. "He's not."

By the time we drive past the small café in Columbia Falls, my stomach has settled, but the seasick queasiness hasn't completely gone away, and I wonder if maybe an infection has somehow settled under one of my scars—maybe below the skin where it can fester and grow without being too noticeable on the surface. I haven't needed my Extra Strength Tylenol until now, and the closer we get to the Wetherelt's, the more I want the bottle in my hand. At just a few miles north of the house, my scars are burning and itching in a way I've not felt before.

At the top of the driveway, Sam stops the truck. My heart is banging so hard I'm certain it might break right through my chest wall. I turn to him. He cups my face in his hands, and I flinch at first, thinking my scars might actually burn his fingers. But instead, the heat subsides and the itching fades, and I can't help but be afraid I've just passed the pain onto him.

"I love you, Melanie," he says, and he kisses me.

"I love you too," I reply.

Sam loves me. He loves me, and I love him, and everything about my life until this moment doesn't matter. It doesn't matter because none of it's real. Clarissa and Decker and Mom and Kurt. Suddenly and unexpectedly, *I'm* real. And I can walk down this driveway and confront Mom, not as the fake me, but as the real me. Melanie Kennicut.

Sam lifts his cell phone into the air. "You call me if you need me. I'm going back to Steve's for the night, but I'll be back here tomorrow. Can't leave the trailer in those trees for too long. Once you've talked to her, maybe she can call off the police."

I nod before kissing him again, and then I stand shakily at the edge of the highway as he drives away. For a moment, the air is still and quiet, like I'm the only person left on the planet, and I can't feel anything—not my hands or my feet or my face. It's as though my soul has left my body, and I'm momentarily suspended between life and death. It's peaceful at first, but then I'm back inside myself and the burning and itching have returned, and with it, a hollowness that seems to swallow me.

Sam. Please come back.

I make my way down the Wetherelt's driveway, the ache in my chest raw enough to take my breath away. At the front door, I grip the handle, my fingers shaking so strongly they cause the thumb latch to rattle. I steady my hand with the other and push the door inward, stepping slowly and quietly into the foyer. Just as carefully, I close the door again behind me.

The house appears empty. All of the lights are off. I hadn't even noticed if the rental Cadillac was parked out front. I place my hand on the banister of the stairway leading to the second floor. The door to the master bedroom is closed. It's late for Mom to be sleeping, but maybe in my absence, maybe in the time she's had to think about me and life, she hasn't slept much. She could be napping. She didn't do it often, but it wasn't impossible.

I consider retreating to my own room to sit and ponder how I'm going to approach Mom when she wakes up, but I don't. I need to do this now, before I change my mind completely, before I let everything prior to yesterday creep back inside and steal me away. When I reach the landing, I step toward the bedroom door, but stop. There are voices on the other side. No, not voices. More like crying. No, not crying either. Moaning. Deep and guttural. As the sounds grow louder, I know what they are.

I open the door to Mom's long copper hair cascading down her naked back. She's on the bed, and beneath her is a body, and from the sounds of the groaning, I know it's a man. But it's not Peter. He must have heard me enter the room because he moves his head across the pillow so he can see me.

"Fuck!" Kurt yells.

Mom swings her head around, her eyes wide and startled like an animal trapped in the headlights of an oncoming vehicle, but instead of remaining still for her impending death the way an animal in those headlights would, she jumps from the bed and comes after me, her right hand striking Kurt in the face as she leaps across the bed.

Her fingers are around my throat and gripping so tightly I can't breathe. She pushes me backwards into the bathroom and against the counter. I'm waiting for her to say something, anything, but she doesn't, and when my eyes meet hers, I don't see anger in them, but rather, fear. She's terrified. When she releases her hands from my neck, she opens her mouth, then closes it again and looks at her fingers. Her body is damp with sweat. A tiny drop of it slips off her chin and onto her naked breasts.

"Joanne!" Kurt yells from the bedroom.

Mom reaches behind me and snatches my cell phone out of the back pocket of my jeans, then turns and exits the bathroom, slamming the door behind her. The doorknob jiggles then steadies as she or Kurt shoves a chair underneath it to prevent me from getting out.

I let the air out of my lungs, aware now I'd been holding my breath since the moment I saw Kurt's face. The shaking begins in my hands, then travels quickly through my body until my legs are trembling uncontrollably and I have to sit on the floor. I wrap my arms around them and drop my forehead onto my knees. Somewhere in that moment between standing and sitting I believe I might suddenly wake up in Sam's arms, beneath the sleeping bag at Steve's cabin. But the longer my knees are pressed into the skin of my forehead, the more I realize this isn't a dream, and the fear that creeps up the length of my spine is just as real. And it's different than any of the childhood fears I've had, like monsters in my closet or the boogeyman under my bed. Those fears are subtle and linger on the surface, easily whisked away when a light is turned on or the closet door is opened. This fear slips beneath that surface and is now settling deep inside my soul.

Voices from the bedroom pull me back out of that place, and I strain to hear the words being spoken. I crawl to the bathroom door and press my ear against it.

"I knew this would happen," Kurt says, anger burning in his throat. "I told you, and you didn't listen. Did you?"

Mom is crying. My cell phone rings.

"Damn it!" Kurt shouts.

There's a thud, and then the cracking and smashing of my phone beneath something heavy. A shoe? A hammer?

Mom is sobbing now.

"You did this on purpose," Kurt says. "Fuck me."

"Please," Mom says. "You need to sober up. You're being irrational."

When Kurt needs to sober up, it means he's high on coke. Feet are shuffling toward the bathroom.

"No," Mom says. "No."

It's the first time in my life I've heard weakness in her voice. Defeat. Fear. I slide away from the door and remain in a crouched position with my back against the cabinets, my arms wrapped around my legs. Kurt yanks the door open and shoves Mom inside, then closes it again and jams the chair back under the knob. For a second, Mom just stares at me, her face red and wet with tears. She's still naked, but the normal elegant stature by which she carries herself is gone. Her skin seems to sag and droop, and her breasts hang heavy. There's a bathrobe hooked on the wall next to the door. She takes it down and wraps it around her body, then sits on the edge of the bathtub, dropping her chin toward her chest. Her hair spills over her face, concealing all but the very top of her forehead. All I can do is look at her long, slender fingers spread out across her knees like spider legs, her manicured nails long enough to scratch a person's eyeballs right out of his head.

What have you done, Mom?

I rise to my feet and sit next to her. She sobs, her hands not moving from their place on her legs. Her head bobs up and down, and with each motion, her back seems to drop lower and lower until she's nearly resting her breasts on the top of her legs, her elbows tucked in toward her stomach. I place my arm over her shoulder, and I pull her to me. She doesn't resist. Her head then falls into my lap, and like a mother to a frightened child, I brush the hair away from her cheek.

-18-

I'm not sure how long I've been stroking Mom's hair before she forces herself back into a sitting position. I barely recognize her beneath smudged mascara, lines of it running down her cheeks like mud trails left behind by inching worms. If I hadn't seen her eyes before she started crying, I would've thought Kurt had been beating her.

"He has a gun, Melanie," she says.

I'm not surprised. Kurt keeps a gun in his office and at his home, and another in his car. He never actually carries one with him—at least I don't think so—but he seems obsessed with the idea that somebody is always trying to "off" him. Mom says it's from the cocaine. When he's high—which is his normal—he's upbeat and smiling, and he talks way too much and too fast, but that's Kurt. It's when he's coming down off the high, right before he hits up again, that he's paranoid. But I've known Kurt for twelve years, and although he's a chauvinistic, arrogant prick most of the time, I've never worried he might be dangerous. He adores Mom and me. He protects us.

I realize now he more than just adores Mom. And I wish I could believe this is the first time, but I know it's not. I've known for a long time, as much as I've tried to convince myself it isn't true. I'd think about Peter, and I'd tell myself Mom loves him. Deep down inside, she really loves him. But I guess she doesn't, and maybe that's why she's never let him be a father to me, why she won't embrace Zach as her son. Peter and Kurt both have money, but Kurt not nearly as much, and he's a part of the world Mom clings to, as am I. And she clings to it for life, like an unborn baby to an umbilical cord.

"What are we going to do?" Mom asks.

I haven't been listening to anything but Mom crying and my own heart beating. I don't know whether Kurt is even still in the house. I stand and press my ear to the door. Nothing. There's one window in the bathroom, on the other side of the Jacuzzi tub, but it's nothing but a large rectangular piece of glass with a view of the lake. There's no way to open it.

"Who builds a bathroom with windows that don't open?" I ask.

Mom doesn't answer. I guess on Flathead Lake in Montana, being locked in a bathroom by a crazy person with a gun is the last thing people worry about. I walk back to the edge of the tub and sit down next to Mom.

"I'm so sorry, Melanie," she says. Her fingers are spread out across her knees again, and she stares at them through puffy, mascara-smeared eyes.

I want to tell her it's not her fault, but it is. "What's he going to do, Mom?"

Sam. Please come back.

She doesn't shift her gaze from her fingers. "I don't know. I've never...never seen this before. I mean, he gets a little weird sometimes when he's been doing coke, but this is different."

Weird isn't really the right word. In my opinion, Kurt is most strange when he's not sniffing the stuff. He's moody and tired and nervous. I remember the fear in Mom's eyes when she shoved me into the bathroom, and a fire begins to burn inside my stomach.

"What are you afraid of, Mom?"

"I...," she drops her face into her hands again and shakes her head.

The heat in my stomach is now making me nauseous. "What?"

Mom takes a deep breath. "He's going to kill me."

I can't help but let out a short laugh.

Kurt? Kill you? Give me a break.

"That's ridiculous." I stand up and press my ear to the door again. I'm trying to pull my own fear out of my soul and back to the surface where I can talk it away. "He's just wacked-out on coke. In a few minutes, he'll figure out what's going on, and he'll let us out of here."

And then what? The three of us will sit down and have a little chat about how I just walked in on them having sex? I'm straining to listen for any sounds from the bedroom, but at the same time, my head is compiling a list of things I want to say to Mom and Kurt, and not so much a list of "things" really, but more like a list of commands. I can't imagine either one of them would want anyone to find out about this. Especially Mom.

I turn back to her, and the heat boils up again in my stomach. I can understand the initial shock of what just happened, but Mom is tough. She'd get over that initial shock soon enough and be up on her feet banging on the door. But instead, tears are spilling down her cheeks, and her hands are shaking against her knees. I swallow back the rising vomit in my throat. Something is very wrong.

"Mom?"

"He's going to kill me," she says. "You don't understand, Melanie."

The woman sitting in front of me is unrecognizable. Weak. Terrified. Suddenly empty of the bitterness and anger and resentment I've had to succumb to my entire life. And it's not just psychological changes taking place before my eyes, but physical ones as well, like I'm witnessing my mother undergoing some kind of strange alien transformation. Her skin is pale and thin, her hair dry and brittle. Beneath the robe, I imagine a withering old woman with bones protruding at odd angles.

"Mom?"

"It was supposed to be an affair," she says. "Kurt knew your father, and I wanted to hurt him. I wanted to show him that I was still good enough for the business. But then Kurt became possessive and controlling, and I tried to leave, but he threatened me. He said he'd ruin me. And you. When I married Peter, I thought he'd get the hint, but that just infuriated him even more. He said he'd kill you and Peter if I stopped seeing him. So, I promised him I'd never leave. But I told him nobody could ever know. Ever. And he agreed. He said if anybody ever found out, he'd kill me…and then himself."

I put my fingers to my lips. I'm not sure why, maybe to assist in the formation of a sentence, or to stop my tongue from falling out of my mouth. I don't know. My scars are tingling, my heart racing, my head a spiraling mess as I try to comprehend Mom's words.

"I didn't believe him at first, about any of it," she says. "But then he picked you up one day when you were eight years old. Do you remember? He came to the house when you were there with Peter and Zach, and he told them you had an audition for a leading role in a Disney series? I was at an appointment."

I can't stand any longer, so I sit down in the middle of the bathroom floor. I do remember that day because it was strange.

Kurt had never taken me to an audition before. Even Peter hesitated at first, but then, it was Kurt. My agent. It made sense he might rush over to walk me into an audition for a leading role at Disney if Mom weren't home to take me. But we never went to the audition. He called Mom when we pulled out of the driveway. He said he had me in the car, and then he said goodbye and hung up. We drove around in circles while he made a few other phone calls, and then he dropped me back off.

"Sorry, Mel," he'd said. "False alarm. The role's been filled."

And then he drove away. Mom came home a few minutes later. Zach and I were watching TV. She ran into the living room, her face red. She was out of breath. Peter asked if she was okay.

"Yes," she replied. "I just didn't feel so good all of a sudden. I'm going upstairs to lie down."

It wasn't particularly unusual behavior for Mom. I watched her hustle up the stairs, and that was that.

Kurt was going to kill me?

"I told him I was through with him, that I couldn't be with him anymore," she says. "After that day, I never did it again. And after awhile, I just came to accept that I was never going to get out. So, I just let it take over my life...and your life. I didn't know what else to do. I couldn't get away, Melanie, and the more I let Kurt control me, the more I didn't want to get away. I know that sounds crazy, so crazy and outrageous, but it's true."

I can't feel my arms and legs, like somehow Mom's monologue just robbed me of all the nerve endings running through those appendages. The burning in my stomach is gone, replaced by something large and heavy as if I just swallowed an enormous stone, and I'm reminded of a show I once saw with Zach about jungle pythons. One of them had eaten an entire goat, and you could see it in the middle of the snake's body like a huge tumor. It wasn't easy taking in something that large, and I couldn't help but feel sorry for the snake, even though the goat was the one who'd just lost its life.

I'm not sure I'm truly grasping the story Mom is telling me. Maybe there's still the remote possibility I'm not really here, that this isn't really happening. But I can't deny the raw connection I have with her right now because I know exactly how she feels. I know what's it like to just accept never being able to get out of something you want so badly to run away from. I know what it's like to let something, or someone, take over your life. And I know what it's like to get to that point where you don't want to run away, where leaving is more terrifying than just sticking it out. And all this time I believed I was the only one suffering. I believed Mom was blaming me for her failed life, that she was using me to fulfill an unfulfilled dream. And even though I don't want to be angry with her right now, I am. I'm pissed she wasn't strong enough to get away, and to take me with her. I'm angry she took everything out on me and made me feel so small and insignificant, when all along she was just as small and just as insignificant.

"When you left yesterday," she says. "When you held that knife to your throat. I didn't know…it was the first time I saw what I'd done to you." A new set of tears pool in her eyes. She blinks, and they race down her red and swollen cheeks, the mascara smudges now washed away. "Kurt was on a midnight flight to Kalispell. I took the knife you had, and I hid it under the mattress. I knew I could stab him, Melanie. If I could just get him in the right position, I could stab him. But then I started thinking about how strong he is, and what if it didn't work. What if he turned the knife on me? So, I looked all over the house for anything else I might be able to use, something easier, and I found a handgun in a case in the storage closet in the garage." She smiles. "And it was loaded. Can you believe it? It was actually loaded."

The odd excitement in Mom's voice causes the stone in my stomach to liquefy and the nausea to return.

"I put the gun on the nightstand," she says. "I knew I'd need to have it close to me. When Kurt saw it last night, I told him I didn't feel safe out here alone, that after you ran off, I searched the house for a weapon. He laughed at me. He said, 'That little thing won't stop a grizzly bear, Joanne.' I could've done it after he fell asleep, Melanie, but I knew it wouldn't make sense that way. It had to look like there was a struggle. And I had it all planned out, but then…then you came in, and…."

I put my hands up in the air. I don't want to hear anymore. I feel like I'm in a movie, and that standing behind me is a director and a cameraman, and Mom's just pulled off the most incredible performance of her career. Any second now, she's going to stand up and a team of makeup artists is going to run to her and reapply the smudged mascara in anticipation of the second take.

Mom sighs. "When you were in your accident, Kurt was convinced you knew something, that you'd done it on purpose to try and pull me away. I had to make sure we scheduled the surgery, Melanie. When you took off yesterday, I called Peter to come up here. I thought if we could find you, the three of us could talk. We could figure out what to do. But he couldn't come, and he didn't know any better, so he called Kurt. And Kurt said you knew. You had to know. Why else would you do this?"

"You never called the police, did you?"

Mom shakes her head. "No."

I inhale a wobbly breath and hold it in my chest for a second. I want it to somehow absorb the acid in my stomach, but it doesn't, and when I let the air back out, I grit my teeth and close my eyes.

"He's going to kill both of us, Mom. And then he's going to kill himself."

She lets her head fall forward as she covers her face with her hands again.

"Yes," she sobs. "Yes."

A voice comes to us from somewhere in the house. Mom's head pops back up. We hold each other's gaze for a moment, and then the voice shatters the silence between us.

Oh no. Oh please.

I jump to my feet and place my hands flat on the door.

"Melanie!" Sam shouts.

I'm afraid to answer back, but if I don't....

"Sam! No, Sam! Get out of here!"

But instead of retreating, heavy feet are running up the stairs and into the bedroom.

"Melanie? What the...?"

"Sam! You have to leave. He has a—"

"Yep." It's Kurt's voice. "I have a gun. And if your little boyfriend here takes one more step toward that bathroom door, I'm going to blow the back of his head off."

-19-

When the bathroom door opens, I want to run into Sam's arms, but Kurt is clutching the bicep of one and pointing the nose of the gun at me.

"Go downstairs," he says as he nods his head toward the bedroom door.

Mom has risen from her seat at the edge of the bathtub and steps up behind me.

"Both of you," he says. "Now."

Sam holds my gaze, his dark eyes void of fear. Instead, he appears completely calm, and more annoyed than anything else. I can't look away from him, but then Mom touches my back, reminding me I need to move.

I make my way down the staircase, Mom right behind me. I turn around for just a split second to make sure Sam and Kurt are taking up the rear. I have no idea what Kurt plans to do with us, but I'm comforted knowing he didn't force Mom and me downstairs while shutting himself and Sam in the bedroom. I can't imagine Kurt would actually let Sam go at this point, but at least he didn't separate him from us in a coke-induced need to remove Sam from the scene altogether.

"On the sofa," Kurt says.

Mom and I sit down. On the coffee table are two lengths of rope and a roll of duct tape. While Mom and I were locked in the bathroom, Kurt must have gone on a mission to find materials. By the look of it, he plans to bind and gag us. What else he's thinking, I don't know, and I don't want to.

"Kurt," Mom says. "Please let the kids go. This isn't about them."

He pushes Sam in the direction of the coffee table. "Give me a piece of that rope."

Sam doesn't move, but then Kurt presses the nose of the gun to the back of his head. "Are you deaf?"

Sam grabs a length of the rope and flips it over his shoulder. Kurt tucks the gun into the lip of his jeans and proceeds to tie Sam's hands behind his back. When he's finished, he pulls Sam to the sofa and places him next to me. I want to wrap my arms around his neck, but he keeps his eyes focused on Kurt, his lips stretched tight, and I know not to embrace him. At first, I think he might be angry, pissed at me for getting him into this mess, but then he moves his head a little, just slightly, and I know it's his way of letting me know he's okay. And I'm okay. Be cool. Everything will be just fine.

But this isn't a movie. I'm not on set. This is as real as it gets, and Kurt is fucked up. And not just from the coke. He's pathological, and he's hit the end of the line. It takes every ounce of strength for me not to reach over and touch Sam's arm. I want to tell him I'm sorry, so incredibly sorry for having disrupted his life. On the other side of me is Mom, her arms crossed over her chest, her head turned toward the French doors and the view of the lake. I want to ask her what she's thinking, but I bite my tongue. Deep down inside, I already know because I'm thinking the same thing. Why didn't I just…?

Kurt grabs me by the wrist and pulls me to my feet. He ties my hands behind my back, and then returns me to the sofa next to Sam. Mom keeps her head turned toward the French doors, as though nothing is happening, and for a second I want to scream at her. But I take several deep breaths instead. She doesn't know how to react to this. The motherly instincts intrinsic in all living species are all but gone in her, shoved way down deep over years of psychological abuse and servitude. Out that window are a lake and blue mountains and trees. In here is something dark and evil and ugly. And right now for Mom, she's had enough of dark and evil and ugly.

With the gun still firmly gripped in one hand, Kurt grabs the duct tape and removes a large strip, placing it over Sam's mouth. He then pulls off another strip and covers mine. Mom hasn't moved. Even when Kurt yanks her to her feet, she keeps her focus on the view beyond the French doors. The normally vibrant green of her eyes has dulled to a grayish blue that reminds me of mold growing on old bread. As Kurt covers her mouth with a strip of duct tape, a tear slips down her cheek and a visible lump forms in her throat.

Kurt pulls her in the direction of the kitchen. When they disappear around the corner, I try to scream through the tape, but the effort instead causes me to swallow the saliva building in my mouth, and I cough violently as I try to catch my breath through my nose. I lean forward, my insides wet and slimy like warm pudding. Sam presses his chest against my back in an effort to hug me or hold me. The feel of his body helps me to slow down my breathing, and when I've finally managed to settle the spasms, I start to cry. I don't know why Kurt has taken Mom away, but I think it's to kill her. To shoot her in the other room so I don't have to watch. I squeeze my eyes shut in an effort to blur the vision of Mom, weak and scared, being shot in the head, but there's no sound of a gun being fired. Instead, they both return to the living room, Mom's hands now tied behind her back as well, and I realize Kurt hadn't expected he'd need three lengths of rope. He went to retrieve a third and took Mom with him to get it so she wouldn't try untying us while he was out of the room.

He puts a strip of duct tape over her mouth, and then seats her back by my side. She turns to me rather than toward the French doors, and I hold her gaze. In her eyes is something foreign. And it's not just because of the moldy green that's now completely devoured the once rich color, like an algae bloom over a quiet pond. Beyond the grayish blue, somewhere deep in Mom's psyche where I can't go, is a closet full of anguish and pain and humiliation, and for so many years, that closet door has been closed to the world. I've never seen anything in Mom's eyes except bitterness and resentment. Toward my father. Toward me. Toward every person in her life who helped strip away her chance of being a recognized figure. But maybe if I'd looked a little closer, I would've seen what I'm seeing now, and I would've tried harder to get to that door and yank it wide open, to expose all of the terrible secrets that had been keeping Mom—and me—prisoner for so long.

Her eyes lift, and I know she's smiling at me, and I make every effort through the tape to smile back. Now, more than ever in my life, I want to reach out and hug her. I want to tell her I love her. I think she wants to do the same, but we can't, so instead, we just keep trying to smile at each other, tears filling both of our eyes, until Kurt pulls Sam and me off the sofa and pushes us toward the French doors. Mom moans through her duct tape, a stifled scream shows through the redness of her cheeks, and my stomach drops hard, giving me the sudden sensation I might pee my pants.

Keeping the gun pointed squarely at my face, Kurt opens the door.

"Out," he says.

Behind us, Mom keeps yelling, her strained voice now rising several octaves as she tries desperately to pull Kurt's attention away from Sam and me. It doesn't work. Once on the deck, he slams the door shut and motions for us to continue walking toward the water's edge. Mom is quiet. Not for lack of trying, but because her voice is now separated from my ears by not only a strip of duct tape, but by a solidly built French door as well. Even if Kurt had left the door open, though, I wouldn't hear Mom above the blood pounding in my ears.

For a moment, Sam is close enough for the heat of his body to touch mine, but then Kurt pulls him away. I don't know if he was trying to comfort me. Maybe he wanted to trip me, to slow the progression of what was likely our destiny—to be gunned down by Kurt, our lifeless bodies then pushed into the water. It makes sense. Based on the size of Flathead Lake, it would take awhile to find us. By then, Kurt would have been given enough time to run off and get lost somewhere in the wilderness, maybe out where Steve lives—remote enough that local roads are closed in the winter. And what about Mom? Why did he leave her in the living room? I try not to think about what he might do to her.

When we reach the shoreline, I take a step further until the water licks my toes. It's bitter cold, but I welcome it. Everything else on my body is burning up. Sam moves up next to me, his shoulder just inches from mine, his eyes as calm as they were in the bedroom, as though we're not walking the plank to our deaths, but rather going on a nice, leisurely afternoon stroll. He turns to me and winks. It's the "we're almost done with this shit" wink I might get from a co-star on a movie set, and it's not funny. The blood bubbles in my ears. But then I realize maybe he's just trying to remain calm for the both of us. Maybe if we act cool and collected, Kurt will stop. If he sees we're afraid, it will only make him more excited. Isn't that what fuels a psychopath? Seeing fear in his victims?

He's pacing behind us now. I can't see him, but he's walking back and forth, his shoes squeaking across the grass. Left to right. Right to left.

"Thought this would be easier," he says. "Fuck."

Left to right. Right to left.

"All I've ever done is love your mother, Melanie. Love her, love her, love her. But do you think she'd give a damn about that? Huh?"

I start to turn around.

"Don't you fucking look at me!" Kurt shouts, and the cold steel of the nose of the gun is suddenly pressed to the back of my head.

My gut burns with the buildup of vomit. It creeps up my throat, but I close my eyes and breathe deeply through my nose. I always thought I'd have flashbacks of my life right before I die—short, sporadic glimpses of the happiest moments of my childhood—but Sam is there instead, the two of us sitting next to each other on Steve's deck, our feet propped up on the deck rail as reds and yellows and purples burst across a dimming sky. The vision pushes the rising vomit back down into my stomach, yanks the fear from my soul so quickly I can almost feel it being ripped out of me, and I suddenly jerk upright, banging the back of my head onto the nose of the gun.

I stand still, waiting for Kurt to pull the trigger, but he backs away from me instead and begins pacing again. Left to right. Right to left. Sam is staring at me, his eyes wide now, the fear in them heavy and solid after witnessing what he and I both thought was my final moment.

"I told her if anybody ever found out, I'd kill her," Kurt says. "You think I'd do that, Melanie? You think I'd kill the woman I love? And then myself? Is she that fucking stupid?"

I don't move my eyes from Sam's. I don't care what Kurt says. If he tells me to look somewhere else, I won't. He can kill me if he wants to, but Sam will be the last face I see before I die.

Kurt is mumbling now, a series of inaudible spasms mixed with fits of laughter. He's delusional, hallucinating. This is good. If we keep still, quiet, maybe he'll just wander off with whatever odd figures his coked-up mind has created. But then he stops his bizarre dialogue and is again right behind me, and even though I promised myself I wouldn't turn away from Sam, I do, because Kurt has the gun pressed to the back of his head instead of mine.

Please. No.

What happens next is as unexpected as a flash of lightning across a cloudless blue sky. Mysterious. Unexplained. The nose of the gun is clearly visible from the corner of my eye, but then it rises sharply, as though Kurt fired it, but there's no sound. No smoke. And Sam is still standing. The quiet is then shattered by voices—yelling and screaming—and when I turn around, there are two bodies rolling across the grass. Sharp sunlight glints off metal. And then there's an ear-splitting bang as the gun goes off, the sound echoing across the lake and scattering for miles in every direction any life that might have been perched in the trees or lingering on the ground.

-20-

I'm not sure how many seconds passed between the gunshot and Kurt grabbing me by the arm and pulling me to his chest, but in that time, Sam fell to his knees and two figures ran out of the house and down the sloping backyard. I can't hear what Mom and Steve are shouting as they near us because there's a loud, steady whistle in my ears like I'm standing next to a fire alarm. On the ground, lying on his back, a growing crimson stain covering his T-shirt, is Joe. As Kurt wraps his arm around my neck and presses the gun to my temple, a thick metallic odor fills my nose and grips my tongue. At first, I think it's just the smell of a gun after being fired, but as it lingers in the back of my throat, I realize it's the scent of blood. Joe's blood.

"Get back!" Kurt yells.

Steve stops briefly, his hands up and at chest level, but then he ignores Kurt and goes to Joe's side. He drops to his knees and presses his fingers to Joe's throat.

"He's alive," he says. He turns to Sam. "He's alive."

Sam's cheeks are red and damp, his eyes burrowed into the bloodstain on Joe's shirt, as though the mess of warm dark red has put some kind of hypnotic trance on him. Steve removes his own

T-shirt and presses it against the gunshot wound on Joe's chest. He pulls his cell phone from his back pocket.

"What the fuck are you doing?" Kurt asks.

Steve pretends not to hear him, but then Kurt tightens his grip around my neck and steps toward Steve with the gun now pointed at him.

"Don't," Kurt says.

Steve's thumb hovers above the phone, his hand shaking.

Mom approaches us, and as she does, Kurt steps away from Steve and turns the gun back on me, the nose of it hot against my temple. Mom's hands are still tied behind her back, the bathrobe clinging to her body, but the duct tape is gone. In its place is a rectangular splotch of irritated red skin where the tape had been pulled free.

"Take me with you," Mom says in a quiet, almost seductive voice. It's the voice I'm most used to hearing—the voice she uses when we're out on auditions or meeting new people or at parties when she's trying to impress the company around her. "Leave her here, Kurt. Take me, and we'll go. We'll run away together."

Kurt backs away, moving toward the house now as Mom follows, pleading with him to let me go. Behind her, Steve keeps his hands pressed to Joe's chest, but he watches us, and now Sam has pulled out of his trance and is watching us too. I don't make eye contact with him. I can't. Lying in a puddle of blood is his father, and he wouldn't be there if it weren't for me.

Kurt stops. Mom has transformed from the terrified, suddenly-aged woman in the upstairs bathroom to the poised, confident person I know her to be. Her moldy-colored eyes have not changed, however, and by this I know she's simply putting on a façade—pretending to want to run away with Kurt in hopes he might let me go.

I try to yell at her through the duct tape on my mouth, and even though there are no words escaping through the thick, fibrous material, Mom knows what I'm saying, but she ignores my efforts to stop her.

"Kurt, my love," she says. "This is our chance to run away. Don't you see that? But we need to go. Now."

"You're a liar," he says. "Why now? After all this time?"

Steve's head is bent, his hand to his ear. He's talking into his cell phone. Mom doesn't move her eyes from Kurt's.

"I was scared," she says. She looks at me. "But not anymore."

Our eyes meet only briefly, but in that moment, something very real and powerful passes between us, like she's just slapped me in the face again, only this time it's out of sincere love for me, the way a parent might strike a small child for running foolishly out into the middle of the road to retrieve a ball. The child cries out in pain and fear, but then is quickly scooped up by the parent who's also crying, but from a pain and fear that is much deeper and much more profound than anything that small child could be feeling from simply being smacked across the face.

Mom looks at Kurt again. "We have to go. If we stay here, we'll never be together."

Kurt's grip on my neck loosens. His body is damp against mine, and as he pushes me away, my skin prickles with gooseflesh with the rush of cool air on the back of my sweat-soaked shirt. I turn around as he grabs Mom by the arm, and then they're running together back into the house. I resist the urge to chase after them, my hands still tied behind my back and my mouth still covered with duct tape, but I let the tears spill from my eyes, my heart swelling in my chest like it's a sponge dropped in water.

I'm about to fall to my knees when Sam's voice reaches my ears, and then his fingers are gripping my arms and he's pulling me into his chest. His hand is on the back of my head as I cry so hard I think I might throw up. He gently pulls the tape from my mouth and presses his lips to mine, and then we're kissing, both of his hands now on my cheeks, the salty taste of his tongue sending a cascade of shivers through my body.

From the front of the house comes the sound of tires on gravel. Kurt and Mom speeding out of the driveway. Sam unties the ropes from my hands, and we hurry to Steve's side, his T-shirt now soaked with as much of Joe's blood as Joe's own shirt. The man's eyes are closed, but a raspy whistle escapes through his parted lips, so I know he's still alive—barely by the amount of blood that has now pooled in the grass around his body. A wave of nausea passes through me.

"Ambulance is on the way," Steve says. He rises to his feet. "You stay here and wait for it. I'm going after them."

"Wait. What?" Sam asks.

As Steve walks between us, I grab his arm.

"Let Sam and me go," I say. "This is my fault."

"This isn't anybody's fault, Melanie," he replies. "But I'm not letting that guy get away. Police here will lose him. I can find him."

He pulls his arm free of my grip, but as he turns to run toward the house, Joe shouts out his name in a gurgling rush of air. Steve hurries back and kneels by his side as Joe manages to lift a hand into the air. Steve takes it in both of his and leans forward until his ear is just above Joe's mouth. After a few seconds, he nods, and then sits back in the grass.

Without looking at Sam and me, Joe's hand still firmly gripped between his, Steve says, "You two go. I'll stay here."

Sam drops to his knees and holds Joe's other hand. "Hang on, Dad. We'll get him. Just hang on."

He kisses him on the forehead before standing up again, and then his fingers are intertwined with mine and we're running around the side of the house to Sam's truck. At the top of the driveway, I tell him to turn right onto the road, assuming Mom and Kurt would have headed back toward Kalispell. If Kurt had no intention of hiding in the woods, he would at least try and make it to the airport.

"Who is he?" Sam asks, his knuckles ghostly white against the steering wheel.

His voice is sharp, bitter. Outside, the sky has begun its evening spectacle of color changing, signifying the end of another day. But this isn't just another day. Back at the Wetherelt's house, a remarkable man lies dying at the edge of the lake, his blood spilled across the grass for no other reason than his son decided to fall in love with a girl from Hollywood whose injuries from a car accident prompted her mother to take her away to a remote place they'd never been. More has happened over the past day and a half than in my entire life so far, and the result is a continuous buzz of energy throughout my body as though every nerve ending has been singularly plugged into a power outlet.

"Melanie?"

"Kurt," I say. "He's my agent."

"Your agent?"

I shake my head, not sure what else to say. He's my agent. A man I've known since I was four years old. A man I thought I knew, but now realize I never actually did. A man with a brain damaged from drugs and a soul twisted by lust and fear who tormented my mother for years until she became someone she didn't recognize. The real Joanne Kennicut disappeared inside herself a long time ago, hidden away in an effort to not hurt the people around her. But in truth, she did hurt those people. Peter and Zach. Me.

"I don't understand, Melanie," Sam says. "Why is he here?"

"It's a long story," I reply. "Let's just find them, and I'll tell you everything. I promise."

He sighs. "Okay."

I stare at his pale knuckles. "Why did you come back to the house?"

Sam loosens his grip on the steering wheel, and as he does, the natural brown of his skin returns to his hands. "I just had a bad feeling. Like when I dropped you off yesterday. Something wasn't right. My chest started to hurt. I was almost to Kalispell when I tried calling you, and when you didn't answer, I phoned Steve and told him I was turning around, that I thought something bad was happening. He said he'd jump in the Jeep and meet me." He shakes his head, tears welling in his eyes. "I told him where to go, but I didn't…I didn't know he was bringing Joe. I didn't expect this."

"He's going to be okay," I say, but my voice shakes. I know it's not true. There was too much blood.

"No he's not, Melanie. He's not going to be okay."

I want to tell him I'm sorry, but I don't. It won't make a difference now. I've been apologizing since I met him, but this is beyond a simple, "I'm sorry," and saying it now would be like throwing gasoline on an already-smoldering fire. Yesterday, I rearranged Sam's daily routine in a way that made it possible for him to bring his father and brother face-to-face for the first time in eight years. It was good. But now, my presence has jolted his world in a way that will alter his life forever, and I can't change that.

Sam releases his foot from the gas pedal. Ahead of us, just around the corner, something is burning. We can't see what it is, but a thick black line of smoke billows into the sky. I place my hands flat on my thighs to try and steady them. Suddenly, we're moving in slow motion. When the truck reaches the bend in the highway, I close my eyes, knowing that what I'm about to see will jolt my world in much the same way my mere presence here has jolted Sam's.

And I'm right. The car is silver and engulfed in flames, the front end smashed into a rock cliff on the other side of the ditch. Traffic is lined up on both sides of the highway. People are standing around, hands on their hips or covering their mouths. Two men appear to be making an effort to get to the driver's side door of the car in hopes of helping whoever is trapped inside.

As we near the accident, I notice another man on his knees, apparently assisting a person lying in the ditch. I jump out of the truck before Sam makes a complete stop. He yells something at me, but I don't hear it. I just run, as fast as I can to the man hunched over Mom.

-21-

I crouch next to the man on his knees. At first, he puts his arm up to stop me, but then he looks at my face and drops his hand back by his side. I don't know why. Maybe it's the pale sheen radiating from my skin or the tears streaming from my eyes, or maybe it's just because the scars startled him. But he doesn't try and stop me again. Instead, he gently places his hand on my shoulder and rises to his feet where he remains standing over Mom and me like a guard.

Before she left the house with Kurt, Mom changed out of the bathrobe and into a pair of her jeans and a white V-neck T-shirt, but there's very little white showing through now. It's brick red instead, like she's been dunked into a giant can of paint. There's blood on her face too, and on her neck and arms. It's all over her, and as I pick up one of her hands and grip it in both of mine, the blood ends up all over me too. I lower my ear to her mouth. She's breathing, but it's shallow and labored. Not far from her head is the gun. Sirens are wailing somewhere off in the distance.

"Driver's dead," a man shouts. "Looks like from a gunshot wound in his neck, though."

Mom squeezes my hand. Her eyes flutter open and she stares at my face.

“I’m here,” I say. “I’m here, Mom.”

The man standing above me mutters something, and then Sam is kneeling by my side.

Mom tries to speak, but I place my fingers on her lips. “Don’t talk. Help is coming.”

Seconds pass. Then minutes. And the whole time, Mom is looking at me, and then something oddly peaceful washes over her face. The emerald green returns to her eyes, and she smiles. She actually smiles, and I’m suddenly remembering a story she once told me, the only thing she ever shared with me about her childhood. I was fourteen years old. She’d been at a party. Kurt drove her home, and when she stumbled through the door, I was in the kitchen getting a bowl of cereal. It was in the middle of the night, and she asked me what I was doing up.

“Can’t sleep,” I’d said. I turned around with my bowl and spoon to head back up to my room, but she stopped me.

“Did I ever tell you about the time my mother took me to a theme park?” she asked. The words slid clumsily across her tongue.

I turned around, surprised she was talking to me about anything other than what happened at the party, who she saw there, and what they were wearing. Mom slumped into one of the bar chairs on the other side of the granite counter.

“I was so scared of that damn roller coaster,” she said. “It was so much bigger than me. And powerful. Oh, was it powerful.”

I set my cereal bowl on the counter, the Frosted Flakes inside of it quickly turning soggy. I didn’t care. This was a rare moment, likely to never happen again, and I was transfixed, and although Mom wasn’t looking at me while she spoke, I knew she wanted me to hear what she was saying.

“I went on some of the smaller stuff,” she said. “The little kids’ rides, but I really wanted to be strong and go on the roller coaster.

I wanted to show my mother that I wasn't scared of it...that nothing could ever control me." She smiled then, but only for a second before a deep frown formed on her lips, as though pieces of string had been attached to each corner of her mouth and someone was pulling down on them.

A heavy, quiet silence filled the room.

The smile returned to Mom's face and she sat up straight. "And I did it. I pushed away all that fear, and I climbed into that seat, and I rode that damn roller coaster." She looked at me then. "And I wasn't scared. That was the happiest day of my life, Melanie. Nobody could touch me." She stared at me for a few seconds, a smile on her face, then slid off the bar chair, grabbed her purse, and stumbled out of the kitchen.

Mom squeezes my hand again.

"The roller coaster," I say.

She smiles, and as the sirens draw closer, she takes a final raspy breath and closes her eyes. I keep her hand clenched between mine, terrified to let it go, even as it gets cold against my skin.

"Mom? Mom?"

Sam puts his hand on my neck, the warmth of his fingers like the first touch of sunlight after days of rain. There are police officers here now and paramedics. The officers escort us away from Mom while the paramedics take our places by her side to try and revive her.

"She's dead," I say, but my voice sounds thousands of miles away, like I'm not really standing here, but rather, I'm way up high in the sky looking down.

Sam's arms are around me. I can't feel them, but I know he's touching me. I know his lips are pressed to my temple too, even though I can't feel them either. I'm aware of the noises around us, all of the people and cars, the trees and grass, the mountains and the lake, even the sky and all that's beyond it. But as the paramedics cease doing CPR on Mom and remove the oxygen mask from her mouth, as they take off their plastic gloves and one checks his watch for the time of death, everything around me seems to disappear into some strange black hole and my body is being crushed by the weight of that hole, like I'm standing in a vacuum-sealed storage bag, and all the air has been sucked out.

I try breathing, but I can't. And then I'm falling into darkness.

When I wake up nearly fifteen hours later, I'm in a hospital bed in Kalispell. Steve is sitting in a chair next to me. I think he's aged another ten years overnight.

"Where's Sam?" I ask.

"This is a lot to comprehend," he replies. "He needed to get some air."

My throat burns.

"Joe's gone," Steve says.

"I know." And I do. As clear as if I'd watched the paramedics stop trying to revive him as I'd seen them do with Mom.

"He knew he was gonna die. That's why he asked me to stay with him. And he knew what was gonna happen. He told me I needed to let you go, that you needed to be there."

I nod.

"You know what's really strange," Steve says. "I think he held on until your mom passed. He knew she'd be scared."

I don't try and stop the tears.

Steve rises from his chair and walks over to the window. Sunlight spills across his face. "Damn old man. Told me to go inside that house. He'd go around back. He knew what he was doing. I'd just pulled the tape off your mom's mouth when I heard the gunshot."

I place my hands on my thighs and spread my fingers out wide. Mom's hands.

Steve walks back and sits at the edge of my bed. "I know you blame yourself for all of this, Melanie. But I think maybe Joe had more to do with it than anyone. He was pulling at the universe, way more than you were, wanting something to happen to make the world shift a little. We all do that now and then. Some people are just stronger."

The roller coaster.

Steve leans forward and kisses me on the forehead.

"I have to run," he says. "They'll take care of you here. Your stepdad's making arrangements for you and your mom's return home."

I wrap my arms around Steve's neck and let my tears soak into his shirt. After he leaves, a number of police officers and investigators come in and out of my room. They ask me questions while writing down the details of what happened at the Wetherelt's house. When they think they've gathered everything they need, they leave, and for a long time I sit alone, hollow and empty, waiting. Mom is gone. Sam does not come to see me.

The following day, I'm driven back to the Wetherelt's house to retrieve our things. There is yellow police tape everywhere, and I'm careful not to touch anything, even though there's no unsolved mystery in what happened. Kurt held us hostage in a cocaine-induced rage. Joe foiled his attempt to kill Sam and me and was accidentally shot in the scuffle. He died later from a single gunshot wound to the chest. And Mom, while sitting next to Kurt in her rented Cadillac, picked up the gun and shot him in the neck while he was driving 70 mph down the highway. Kurt was wearing a seatbelt. Mom wasn't, but because of the angle of her body when the car careened off the road and hit the rock wall, she was miraculously not thrown from the vehicle. She managed to crawl out of the burning wreckage where she died of massive internal bleeding…while holding my hand.

The roller coaster.

I pack my suitcase first, then Mom's. As I put her clothes in her bag, my knees begin to wobble and a rock lodges in my throat. I shove the remaining items into the suitcase and slam it shut, then sit on the edge of the bed and cry—deep, heavy sobs that threaten to shatter my bones.

At the airport later, an employee of the company Peter's firm hired to fly up and get me escorts me to a private jet. Mom's body is somewhere in that jet. Down below in the cold, wrapped in a black thermal body bag, and enclosed in a temporary casket. Kurt's family arranged for the return of his body separately. Peter knows where to bury Mom. She once mentioned to him that when she dies, she wants her final resting place to be at Forest Lawn Memorial Park where lots of famous people have been laid to rest. But that doesn't seem so fitting anymore. I think maybe that's where Kurt will go, so I'll make sure Mom is taken somewhere else. Maybe in Malibu by the ocean.

As I board the plane, I look back down toward the main portion of the airport where a long length of windows gives people on the inside a view of their loved ones taking off and landing. Even if I were closer to those windows, I wouldn't be able to see the faces behind them. But I know Sam isn't in there anyway. Just before I step inside the jet, I steal another quick glance at the doors, hoping he might come running through them to chase me down and wrap his arms around me. Tell me everything will be okay. And kiss me. Kiss me.

I drift in and out of sleep on the flight back to Los Angeles, and in that sleep is a slide show of recent memories—the feel of

Sam's fingers tracing my scars, his hands on my skin beneath the sleeping bag at Steve's, and then Mom's naked body standing before me, the sickly green of her eyes, and Kurt's breath in my ear. I wake up to the sound of a gunshot and the crunch of metal against jagged rock, and then the plane is falling. Falling. When the wheels touch the runway, I release the air in my lungs and wipe the sweat from my brow.

The jet comes to a complete stop, and the flight attendant opens the door. She smiles at me as I disembark—a sad smile, thin and tight and curved at the edges like she's sucking on a lemon. At the bottom of the stairs is Peter, his eyes hidden behind dark sunglasses. He's wearing khaki shorts and a black T-shirt. As I make my way down the steps, I suddenly feel like I'm melting, like I'm a soft piece of candy stuck on blacktop beneath a hot summer sun. At the bottom of the stairs, Peter steps toward me, and I fall into his chest in a spasm of painful sobs.

-22-

Mom was buried in Malibu, in a small cemetery overlooking the ocean. Edie, one of Mom's girlfriends from the area, told Peter it was where Mom would have wanted to be laid to rest. It was quiet up there, peaceful. And from that point, she could witness the miracle of endless sunsets, something she apparently loved to do with Edie. They'd meet for gin and tonics, and while watching the sun slip below the horizon, taking with it the day's blend of oranges and reds and yellows, Mom would confess many things to Edie.

"I should've told somebody," she said to me on the day of Mom's funeral. "But I promised to keep it just between the two of us. She made me promise. And to be honest with you, Melanie, I wasn't sure how much of it was true, especially after a few drinks."

I'd never met Edie before that day. I'd never even heard of her. Mom's other friends from Malibu were at the service as well—Celeste and Sharon and Deborah Hellerman. But Edie didn't know any of them.

"Your mom and I were friends when we were kids," she said. "She started modeling near the end of eighth grade. I didn't see her much after that, but I'd heard from other people that she wasn't the same person, that the business was changing her. And then about four years ago, right after I moved to Malibu with my husband, I ran into her on the street. She'd just finished having lunch with her girlfriends. We grabbed coffee and caught up. After that, we got together just about every week."

Mom went to Malibu on Saturdays to have lunch with "the girls." But Celeste and Sharon both told me they hadn't seen Mom much over the past few years.

"She just stopped coming," Celeste said. "Every now and then, she'd show up, but I think the last time I saw her was almost two years ago."

Instead of lunch, Mom had been meeting Edie at a tiny beach surfer bar north of Malibu—the Rusty Gull. A dive bar, according to Edie. A place I'd never imagine Mom stepping foot inside of, and learning she'd been spending time there just about every Saturday for the past few years made me smile.

"I guess I was her escape," Edie said. "We'd talk about being kids for awhile, and then after a few gin and tonics, she'd tell me all about you and your career. She loved you, Melanie, but every time your name came up, she'd get sad. After a few months, she told me about Kurt and what was happening. She said as soon as you turned eighteen, she was going to stop." Edie started crying then. "I wish I'd done something for her."

But there wasn't anything anybody could do. And truthfully, it seems Edie did more for Mom than any one person could have. She listened. Mom would go to the Rusty Gull and step outside of the nightmare of her life, even for just a few hours, and then she'd step back in. For four years, she had a weekly escape—one that made it possible for her to return to the terror, but with a shred of light at the end of the tunnel—her Saturday drinks with Edie.

The service was short and lightly attended. The only other people there aside from Edie, Celeste, Sharon, and Deborah were a handful of Peter's colleagues, most of which I'm not even sure knew Mom that well. But they came to console Peter. I was sad to see how few faces there were. I remember someone once saying you can tell how a person lived his or her life by the number of folks who attend that person's funeral. Mom stopped living her life a long time ago.

At the reception after, I wandered outside. The hall was a short walking distance from a cliff overlooking the ocean. Gulls and pelicans drifted up and down along the skyline. I stood at the edge of that cliff and gazed out at the endless expanse of water, as blue as I'd ever seen it. I thought about Flathead Lake.

Sam.

Ten days had passed since I left Montana, and I hadn't heard from him. I tried calling a few times, but he didn't answer, and I didn't leave messages.

After the funeral reception as I was walking back to the car with Peter and Zach, Edie walked up to me and gave me a hug.

"I'm here for you if you need me," she said.

As she turned around to leave, I asked if Mom had ever said anything about my father.

"Donald Crowder," she replied. "That's all I know."

And that's all I needed to know. Mom had never once spoken his name.

It's Tuesday, three days after Mom's service, and my hands are shaking. Peter is sitting across from me at the dining room table. Zach is at a friend's house for the afternoon. I'd been waiting to talk to Peter about Mom until enough time had passed. Two weeks seems adequate, but when I look at Peter's eyes now, my throat squeezes shut.

When I first arrived home, he had a barrage of questions about what had happened at Gordon Wetherelt's house. From the police, he learned the bare minimum—that Kurt had been high on coke and had held Mom and me hostage before releasing me and taking her in a foiled kidnapping attempt that ended in both of their deaths. He knew nothing about what I'd witnessed in the bedroom and nothing about Mom's tormented and deadly affair with Kurt. At the time, I didn't have the heart to say anything. Instead, I told him about Sam and Joe and Steve. And he let me cry.

Even now as I sit across from Peter, there's a dark emptiness inside me I'm certain will never go away. By telling him about Mom and Kurt—the type of secret one would want to take to his or her grave—I hope some of that darkness will go away. I could keep the truth concealed for the rest of my life, and in that way protect Peter from the pain it would undoubtedly cause, but I know in my heart it's not what Mom would want me to do. With Edie, she had an unbiased source to confess her pain and guilt to, a person who knew her long before the noxious weeds of Hollywood contaminated her soul. In time, Mom would've found a way to tell Peter, but she's gone now. I'm all that's left of her.

Pushed against the far wall of the dining room is the grandfather clock once owned by Peter's mother. The second hand ticks loudly, and I think about Mom's fingernails clicking across the mahogany table the day Clarissa stood outside our front door. It seems an entire lifetime has passed since then. I remember Mom's face—eyes wide, skin pale and taut, her bottom lip quivering. Anger? Fear? I thought I knew. But I didn't. I crawled into her head that day, and I saw panic, but not panic for the reasons I believed. And I know I'll spend the rest of my life recalling things Mom said and did and wishing I'd known her the way I know her now.

"I have something to tell you," I say, my voice like a trumpet.

Peter leans forward. He rests his elbows on the table and crosses his fingers in front of his face. His eyes are heavy and sad.

"Mom and Kurt…."

Peter nods.

"But it's not what you think," I say. "Mom didn't love him. She was protecting us."

Listening to my own words, I realize how ridiculous it must sound to Peter. I want him to respond, but he doesn't. He waits, and suddenly I can't talk, like I've just swallowed a piece of cotton. And I wonder if it's worth it. What he doesn't know can't hurt him.

"I know, Melanie," he says. "I've known for a long time."

I fold my hands together on the table. "It's worse than you think, Peter."

His body stiffens, but as I proceed to tell him everything, his shoulders sag and his head drops, and then he's crying, deep and heavy. At one point, he bangs a fist against the table, his cheeks red and his jaw tight, but then he crumples forward and tears fall from the tip of his chin like a leaky water faucet. When I've shared with him everything I know and everything Edie told me, I'm exhausted and my muscles ache, as though I've just finished running a short marathon.

"I didn't know," Peter says. "I should've, but I didn't. I'm an attorney for God's sake, I could've helped her."

We sit in silence for a few minutes, the ticking of the grandfather clock reminding us that the world is still spinning, that we're both still alive and needing to pick up the pieces and move on. Sam drifts through my mind, and then my heart, and an ache creeps into the deepest part of me and lingers there until I have no choice but to hang my head and weep. I long to feel his arms around me, his lips on mine. And then I long to hear Mom's voice, to see the deep green of her eyes. But they're both gone.

Peter walks around the dining room table and sits down next to me. He puts his arm over my shoulder, and I lean into his chest. His T-shirt is damp and smells of cologne.

"So, what do we do now?" he says.

His heart is beating slow and gentle and quiet, like soft music in my ear, and I strain to keep my eyes open. When Zach was little and he'd fall asleep on the sofa in the living room, Peter used to carry him to bed. I always wondered what that would feel like, so one night after he'd brought Zach upstairs, I pretended to fall asleep myself, hoping he'd carry me to my room as well. When he came back downstairs, he stood for a long time at the edge of the sofa, maybe contemplating whether to scoop me into his arms. My body screamed for his touch, but he covered me with a blanket instead and disappeared up the stairs.

Peter's arms are around me, and then he's lifting me from my chair, my head still pressed against his chest. I'm floating and drifting and spinning all at the same time, and then I'm being lowered onto my bed. Peter's lips are on my face, kissing the scar on my cheek.

"You're my beautiful girl," he whispers. And I fall asleep.

-23-

I let another week pass before I try calling Sam again. This time, my call is answered, but it's not Sam on the other end of the line.

"Hi Melanie."

"Steve?"

"Yep. It's me, sweetheart."

Even though it's not Sam saying these words, my skin comes alive.

"How are you?" Steve asks.

"I'm okay," I reply.

"Are you? Really?"

I want to say yes, but I can't. I clench my teeth together, hoping I can find my voice and use it without shaking.

"I'm so sorry, Melanie," Steve says.

And then I'm crying. He waits quietly on the other end of the phone until I'm able to catch my breath.

"How are you?" I ask.

"Hanging in there," he replies. "We've been trying to organize all of Joe's stuff. The tribe held a service for him. It was amazing. I think the entire Salish Kootenai nation was there." He laughs. I think about the few people who came to Mom's funeral. "He wanted the tribe to take control of his property, use it to house another family, so we've been cleaning it up as best we can."

"And how's Sam?" I ask, my chest aching.

After a brief pause, Steve says, "I guess he's okay. Confused, I think. We've been so busy putting everything in order, there hasn't been much time to think about anything else."

He's trying to be nice, but I know no matter how much there is to do, you can still think about a person, and you can still pick up the phone and dial someone's number.

"He's coming back to the cabin with me when we're done here," Steve says. "For now. Not sure what we're gonna do after that."

"Does he...ever say anything? About me?"

Silence, and then, "I think this will just take some time, Melanie. There's so much hurt right now. And guilt. Lots of guilt."

"Okay," I say. "Will you just...tell him I called?"

"Of course," Steve replies.

We say goodbye and hang up. I think Sam is sitting across from Steve, and I wonder what they're saying to each other now, if Steve is telling Sam to call me. I hope he is. On my bedside table is a Post-it Note with an address scribbled in black pen. I pick it up and stare at the numbers and letters, my stomach doing a quick somersault.

In the kitchen, Peter left the keys to Mom's Cadillac. I don't need a car like hers, but I'm not ready to get rid of it. Everything else of Mom's that has monetary or sentimental value, we packed up in boxes. Someday when I'm ready to go through it, I will, but I don't know when that day will come. Maybe never.

I pull out of the driveway and make my way toward Beverly Hills, the Post-it Note now stuck on the steering wheel, the black letters and numbers blinking at me as I drive beneath the flickering shadows of palm trees. By the time I reach the address on the note, my hands are glued to the Cadillac's steering wheel. I turn into an underground parking garage. The valet is a young man with dark hair and light eyes. When I step from the car, he's behind me, and I know he's smiling. But when I turn around to face him, the smile vanishes, and he looks down at my hands as I give him the key. He doesn't look up again.

At the elevator, two women move away from me, and when the door opens, an older gentleman exits and walks between us. I step inside and turn around, expecting the women to be right behind me, but they're gone. As the elevator door closes, I ignore the painful gnawing in my throat and chest. I know this is how it will be. Now, and possibly forever. Tomorrow, I have an appointment with Dr. Levington, my first follow-up since before I left for Montana. He'll be able to tell me whether we can keep the scheduled surgery date or move it up.

When the elevator door opens again, I step into a dimly-lit hallway. Up and down each side are closed doors, each displaying a plaque with the name of a person or persons or company etched on it. At the end of the hallway is a single door. The plaque on that one reads, "Twisted Pony Productions." I wrap my fingers around the brass doorknob and turn it to the right. It's unlocked. I take a deep breath and walk into the office.

The waiting room is small, but elegantly decorated—hardwood floors and beige walls, a soft brown leather sofa and matching love seat, and a round glass table in the middle of the room with a giant vase full of calla lilies placed in its center. There's a receptionist desk on the other side of the room. Behind it sits a young woman with curly red hair and a petite nose, her lipstick a pale shade of pink. She forces a smile as I walk toward her.

"How may I help you?" she asks, trying to keep her eyes on mine, but with little success. She keeps looking at my forehead, then my cheek.

"I'm here to see Donald Crowder," I reply.

"Is he expecting you?" Forehead. Cheek. Eyes. Forehead.

"No, but a mutual friend has passed away, and I need to let him know."

She wrinkles her tiny nose, either because she's confused by my request or because she's pretending to feel sorry for me.

"My condolences," she says quietly. She picks up the telephone receiver and presses a button. "Mr. Crowder? There's a young woman here asking to see you." She looks at me and smiles. "No. I don't think so. She says a mutual friend has passed away, and.... Okay." She hangs up the phone. "He'll be right out."

"Thank you," I say.

I turn around, my heart rattling like it's full of tiny pebbles. On the drive to Donald's office, in the elevator, even just now as I stood in front of his receptionist, I held the possibility in my head he wouldn't be here, and that possibility kept me from getting sucked into a tornado of anger and fear and sadness. But that tornado is spinning now, twisting and spiraling and building momentum.

I sit at the edge of the leather sofa and squeeze my hands between my knees as I try to steady my breathing. A door next to the reception desk opens and a man steps out. At first, I can't move my eyes from his shoes—shiny black loafers with a crisscross woven pattern—until he's walked to the corner of the sofa, and then I stand and look at his face. His eyes are dark, his hair mostly gray. He combs it over in an attempt to cover his balding head. He's wearing a pair of thin reading glasses attached to a lanyard around his neck. He removes the glasses from his face and drops them to his chest. His nose is big and red and bulbous. During one of Mrs. Orton's science lessons about the human body, she told Clarissa and me that severe alcoholism can sometimes lead to what is called rhinophyma.

"As the condition of the liver deteriorates with advancing alcoholism, its ability to deal with fats in the blood decreases," she'd said. "The extra fat is deposited beneath the skin in areas with a lot of sebaceous glands. Since the skin in the nose is both thin across the cartilage and also has a lot of glands, the buildup there actually changes the shape of the nose."

She then showed us a few sample photos of men and women suffering from rhinophyma. Clarissa touched her own nose, then looked at me, her eyes wide with panic. But Mrs. Orton's lesson did nothing to change how many screwdrivers she drank the following evening at her agency's Halloween party. Dressed as Dorothy from *The Wizard of Oz,* Clarissa threw up all over her ruby red shoes, and then tossed them into the swimming pool along with a little basket carrying a stuffed Toto. In the morning, she called me in tears because she'd paid over $400 for those ruby red shoes.

"I'm sorry," Donald says. "Do I know you?"

I'm staring at his bulbous nose. And he's staring at my scars. I want to laugh.

"Uh…Patty mentioned a death." He turns to Patty. She shrugs her shoulders.

I clench my hands into fists. "Yes. Joanne Kennicut. She died in a car accident."

Donald crosses his arms over his chest. "Joanne Kennicut?" He shakes his head. "I don't know anyone by that name."

Of course you don't.

I don't know what Mom saw in Donald Crowder. He's tall and relatively thin. Maybe twenty years ago he was handsome, before losing his hair and before his nose transformed into some kind of grotesque alien life form. He has good taste in shoes. Nice slacks. But the white, long-sleeved turtleneck—too tight against his aging chest—has to go.

"But you know me, right?" I ask.

Donald takes a step back. He cups his chin in one hand and studies my face. "I...you look sort of familiar, I guess."

I unclench my fists and straighten my back until I'm standing as tall as I'm able to, my eyes level with his mouth. "Look at me."

"Miss," he says. "I'm really busy. You're interrupting my day. You found your way in, now find your way back out." He turns around and walks toward Patty.

"I'm your daughter," I say.

Donald stops. Patty gasps. He spins around and takes two steps in my direction.

"Now you listen to me," he says. "If I had a dime every time some young broad came in here trying to pull one on me, I'd be a damn millionaire. Hollywood's a bitch, honey. Get used to it. And with that face, I'm sorry, but you don't have a chance. Can't wrap your legs around any of us for a job, so you waltz on in and act like I'm your damn daddy. Get the hell out of here." He points to the door. Behind him, Patty pretends to be talking on the telephone.

"You had an affair with Joanne Kennicut," I say, my voice wobbly. "She got pregnant with me. You dumped her. My name is Melanie Kennicut. I'm a model and an actress. My agent is...was Kurt Adams."

"Kurt Adams is dead," Donald says.

I nod. "I know. My mother killed him."

Donald steps away from me. "This is insane."

Patty is no longer pretending to be on the telephone. She's staring at the computer screen in front of her. I'm guessing she's looking me up on IMDb—the Internet movie database system. Most working actors have a profile. Her eyes widen. She looks at me, then back at the computer, then at me again.

"I just thought you should know," I say. "My mother was a good person. I'm sorry you don't remember her."

I turn around and walk back into the hallway. As the door closes behind me, Donald says my name, but I don't return to his office. I won't see him again. In the elevator, I place my hands on my stomach. I don't know how I thought I'd feel if I saw him. I didn't have a script written. I only knew in my heart I needed to tell him about Mom. Now I wonder why. He doesn't remember her anyway, and he doesn't know me. But as I step off the elevator and wait for the valet to bring Mom's car around, the tornado inside of me begins to unravel and weaken. By the time I pull out of the garage, it's fallen apart altogether, and as I drive home, I have the strange sensation Mom's with me, sitting in the passenger seat smiling at the sun.

-24-

"You've healed up nicely," Dr. Levington says. He's sitting at his desk across from Peter and me. "We can keep the scheduled date as is, but I don't see any reason why we can't do it earlier."

After my meeting with Donald Crowder yesterday, I came home and told Peter I didn't want to go through with the surgery. I wanted to move forward, as I am now. Stronger. More confident. He didn't say a word as I rambled. He just smiled his awkward smile.

"What happens if she doesn't do it?" Peter asks.

Dr. Levington cocks his head. "I...didn't know that was an option."

I take the hand mirror from the edge of his desk and hold it up so I can look at my face. The scars are just scars now, not so red and fleshy anymore, and no longer ugly to me. Underneath them is a girl I don't recognize, a girl I don't know. Before Montana, before Sam, I was terrified of being anybody but that girl. Who am I if I'm not beautiful? But now I know I can be the person I want, pretty face or not, and knowing this, knowing there's a world out there where people—like Sam—can love me for what I am inside, has given me the crazy notion I've been reborn. I've been given a second chance to live the life I want to live.

Dr. Levington leans forward. "Are you sure, Melanie? What about your career?"

Donald's words ring in my ears. *And with that face, I'm sorry, but you don't have a chance.*

"Yes," I reply.

Dr. Levington looks at Peter. "Must be a rebellious teenager thing. You going to help me out here, Pete?"

Peter smiles. "Nope."

Dr. Levington turns to me. "Okay, then. But if you change your mind, Melanie, call me." He puts his hands in the air and flips them back and forth. "These are magical. Take your time. Doesn't matter how long you wait, I can make you beautiful again."

Zach is starting middle school in just over two weeks, so Peter decided it was time to have a final summer barbecue. It's my official first with them, and although I try to mingle with Peter's friends during it, I find myself exhausted from trying to skirt around conversations about my career and my accident, and then Mom. I can't shake the feeling they're all trying just a little too hard.

Zach and his friends are swimming in the pool. He introduced me to them, and they were all very nice, but in their retreat back into the water to finish their game of Marco Polo, I heard one of them ask Zach if I was ever going to get to be a model again.

"She was so hot," he said.

I move away from the party and find a quiet spot in one of Peter's lounge chairs on the patio. My cell phone is in my hand. I want to call Sam. I miss him so much it hurts. I've heard the cliché before, but now I know how it feels. Raw and cold and empty, like my blood and bones have been sucked away and all I'm left with is my sagging skin and aching stomach.

In the sky above, stars are muted and fuzzy, faded behind an invisible cloud of smog and the glow of city lights. During the week in Montana before I left with Sam, there were a few nights after Mom had gone to bed when I walked to the end of the Wetherelt's dock and I lay on my back to stare at the sky. The stars were so bright there, I could make out every constellation without having to search or squint, and their reflection on the lake produced an entirely new universe, as though another set of stars lay just below the surface of the water. I would gaze at the stars in the sky until my back became as stiff as the dock beneath it, and then I'd drag myself to the house, hoping Sam would return in the morning to tend to the Wetherelt's yard. Just like those stars, he moved me.

Peter waves from his spot in front of the barbecue. I wave back. He closes the lid and hands his tongs to Earl Mariner, one of the attorneys Peter works with at the firm. I'm glad he's coming to talk to me, to see if I'm okay, to find out if I need anything. I guess he feels like he has to make up for all the years he had to ignore me. But I'm also sad for him. I don't want him to spend the rest of his life feeling like he has to take care of me, that because he couldn't be the father to me he wanted to, he now has to change the direction of his life, whatever direction that is.

Peter grabs the second lounge chair and pulls it up next to me, then falls into it and sighs. "Not such a bad night, is it?"

"It's great, Peter. Thanks."

We sit in silence for a few seconds.

"I finalized all of the paperwork for your mom's policy," he says.

I nod. I didn't know Mom had a life insurance policy worth $3,000,000. Only Peter knew, and he'd made sure I was the only beneficiary of it. It's being held for me until I turn eighteen, at which time all of my earnings for the past thirteen years will also be released. But it doesn't make a difference.

"Have you talked to Mrs. Orton?" he asks.

"Yeah. She said I can come back whenever I'm ready."

"And?"

"I will. Soon."

Silence.

"You know," Peter says, "I was thinking." He leans forward in his lounge chair. "I have a little down time over the next few weeks." He turns to me. "I can make arrangements for Zach." He pauses.

"Yes?"

"Maybe you and I should take that trip I promised."

"You mean...."

"Yeah." Peter smiles. "Paris."

Four days later, Zach and I are walking through the Beverly Center on a shopping spree for his new school clothes when Clarissa and Juliette appear from around the corner. I consider grabbing Zach and running into the nearest store, but I don't. Instead, I move directly toward Clarissa, and when her eyes meet mine, I hold them and don't stop moving until I'm standing directly in front of her.

"Melanie," Juliette says. She wraps her arms around me and squeezes. "I've been meaning to call Peter. I'm so, so sorry about your mother. It's such a tragedy. Such a terrible tragedy."

I keep my eyes on Clarissa. She's looking at the ground.

I turn to Zach. "Why don't you go ahead to Lids? I'll meet you there."

"Okay," he says. "Hi Clarissa."

She nods her head a little, but doesn't look at him.

"I won't be long," I say to Zach as he walks away.

Mom and Juliette didn't remain friends after we all met, but I still thought she would've made some kind of effort to contact me when the news of Mom's death got around. But that would require a heart, and I don't think Juliette has one.

"How are you holding up?" she asks.

My skin is suddenly hot. "Are you asking me that because you really want to know or because you don't know what else to say?"

She blushes. "Well…I…." She turns to Clarissa. "I'll just leave you girls alone for a bit." And she walks away.

It's just Clarissa and me now, and neither of us knows what to say, and for the first time in ten years, I don't really care if she says anything at all. In fact, I can't even remember what her voice sounds like. Standing across from her, I realize we have absolutely nothing in common, and we never did. The day she brought Decker to my house, I thought my life was over. Now I realize, it was just beginning. Clarissa is nothing but a reminder of who I didn't want to be. I knew it then, and I feel it now, like the sun breaking through the clouds.

"Bye Clarissa," I say, and I walk past her.

Like Donald, she says my name, but I don't turn back. And I won't see her again either. Not her. Not Juliette. Not Decker. They're characters in a television show that's no longer on the air, and like watching old reruns, I might visit them again, but only when reminiscing about the past.

Zach and I leave Beverly Center and drive to Malibu to visit Mom's grave. I stop at a market on the way to buy an arrangement of summer flowers—dahlias and asters and yellow daisies. By the time we get to the cemetery, the sun is setting and Mom's white granite tombstone is showered in a blazing mix of vibrant yellows and reds. I place the flowers at the base of the stone and step back to watch the fiery colors dance across her name—Joanne Marie Kennicut.

When I turn to Zach, there are tears in his eyes.

"I didn't really know her, Mel," he says. "And I'm sorry about that."

I put my arm over his shoulder. "I didn't either, Zach. But it's not your fault. She didn't really even know herself."

"I wish sometimes we could just go back and start over, you know."

"Yeah," I say. "I know. But we have something even better."

He looks at me, his brow furrowed. "Like what?"

I stare out across the ocean. "We have tomorrow."

The sun slips beyond the horizon, and like baby animals following their mother into the safety of their den, the colors drift away from Mom's tombstone and disappear with the setting sun.

-25-

It's the morning before our scheduled flight to Paris, and Peter gives me the bad news.

"I'm so sorry, Mel," he says. "I have to fill in for this case. It's just one of those attorney obligations, and I'm not comfortable letting anyone else in the firm do it. But it's only for two days. I'll meet you there."

"You mean, I should go without you?" It's a ridiculous question. I could wait and go with Peter, but then he has to pay for two ticket changes, and we lose the money for the nights we're not staying in the hotel he booked. And it's Paris. We only have six days there. Based on the travel book we bought, that's barely enough time to see a quarter of the city.

"I think you can manage," he says, smiling. "I've been to the Louvre and Notre Dame. You could see both of those before I get there, and then we can do everything else after I arrive."

"But I've never gone anywhere by myself," I say. "And this is a big deal. I've never been out of the country. I have no idea what I'm supposed to do."

"You're seventeen, Melanie," Peter replies. "It's about time. It's just two days. You get on the plane. Get off the plane. Tell the cab driver to take you to Hotel Duo, 11 Rue du Temple. Notre Dame and the Louvre are walking distance from there."

"Didn't you ever see *Taken?*" I ask.

Peter reaches across the granite counter and places his hands over mine. "Just don't share a cab with anybody."

"Not funny."

He smiles. "I have to run."

I spend the rest of the afternoon packing for the trip—shorts and T-shirts and casual summer dresses, one evening dress (Peter's request), and a pair of black strappy sandals. When my suitcase is closed and ready to go, I sit on my bed and review the travel book, highlighting the places I want to see. The Eiffel Tower, Versailles, the Arc de Triomphe, Montmartre. The book is filled with photographs of couples walking hand in hand, drinking wine by the River Seine, kissing on a park bench beneath weeping willows. Paris is known for being the most romantic city in the world. Mrs. Orton even told me it's most appreciated when visited with a love.

"And not just any love," she'd said. "Your one true love. The love of your life."

I close the travel book and tuck it into my carry-on bag. My cell phone is resting on my bedside table. I consider calling Sam. But I don't. By now, he and Steve are back at Steve's cabin, and he's moving on with his life in much the same way I'm moving on with mine. As difficult as it's been, I've accepted that he's chosen to let me go. The hours we spent together were the most amazing of my life, and I think they were for him too. I think. But what happened to Joe can't be changed. There's no amount of apologizing that can bring him back, and I will always be a symbol of pain for Sam. A reminder of what he's lost, not of what he's gained.

The following day, Peter drives me to LAX. In the car, we review over and over and over again what I'm supposed to do when I get to Charles de Gaulle. He explains the layout of the airport to me, the customs process, where to catch a cab.

"Don't worry," he says, "the drivers all speak English."

I make a joke about how my scars might scare them all away, like the Elephant Man, but Peter is not amused.

"That's London, not Paris," he says, and we both laugh.

At the airport, he parks the car.

"You could've just dropped me off," I say.

"Not a chance."

Through the parking garage and across the street leading to the Tom Bradley International Terminal, Peter watches people. He stares at those who appear to be following me with their eyes, and to one woman, he says, "Take a picture. It lasts longer." Before the accident when Peter and I would be out together, which wasn't very often, he'd make similar comments to the men who couldn't keep from gawking at me, but this is different. There's a definite change in the tone of his voice. Back then, there was a hint of humor beneath the hostility. But now, the humor is gone.

We check my suitcase and retrieve my boarding pass. I put my passport back into my purse. Fortunately, I've had one since I was fifteen when the possibility of modeling in Japan presented itself. But Kurt wouldn't allow it. I didn't understand why back then, but I do now.

At the first security checkpoint, Peter gives me a hug. When he backs away, there are tears in his eyes.

"I'm fine, Peter," I say. "This doesn't bother me. People staring at me, I mean."

He nods. "I just…I don't know."

"I'll see you in two days."

He hugs me again, then turns and walks away. As he disappears around the corner, my stomach flutters. I'm nervous about traveling alone to a foreign country, about the uncomfortable stares I'm getting now and will be getting when I arrive in Paris. I don't know how to speak French. I don't really know where I'm going or how I'm getting there. But the queasiness now has less to do with those nerves and more to do with the bizarre thought in my head that Peter isn't going to meet me, that he's sent me out on some odd adventure he hopes will cure me of my heartache.

I shake the thought from my head and step into line.

I arrive in Paris at 11:35 a.m. It was an overnight direct flight, so I was able to sleep through much of it. I follow Peter's instructions about customs and immigration and the baggage claim. On my way to the cab line, I buy the international phone card he recommended, and I wake him up in the middle of the night to let him know I arrived.

"Great," he says, his voice froggy. "Call me before you go to bed."

The cab driver gives me a wry smile, but when I say where I'm from, he proceeds to tell me all about his famous movie-star brother, a man I've never heard of before. I don't listen to most of what he's saying because outside the cab is Paris, and I find it impossible to pull my eyes away from its grandeur.

It isn't until I've checked in at the Hotel Duo that the exhaustion hits me. I fall on the bed—too tired to care the room has one double bed instead of two singles—and close my eyes. Just for a minute, I think, but then I'm back in Montana, standing at the edge of the lake, tiny ripples of icy water teasing my toes. The air is quiet except for the wind whispering through the trees. At first, I think I'm alone, but then there are arms around me, thick and strong, and they pull me back until I'm pressed against the warmth of someone's chest. He kisses my ear, then my neck. My body goes limp, and my legs wobble. I turn around slowly and touch my lips to Sam's.

Sam.

A telephone is ringing. I'm confused at first about where I am, but then the fog of sleep lifts and I remember I'm in Paris, in a room at the Hotel Duo. I grab the phone.

"Hello?"

"Pardon, Ms. Kennicut, for a call." The woman has a thick French accent. There's a click on the other end of the line, and then voices—Zach and Peter talking to each other.

"Hello?"

"Hi Mel," Peter says. "Just wanted to make sure you got to the room okay."

I scoot to the edge of the bed and swing my legs over the side of it. "Yep. It's really nice, Peter."

"You sound tired."

"A little. I was just taking a nap."

"Oh shoot, did I wake you?"

"It's okay," I say. "Is everything all right?"

"Yes, yes," he replies. "I'm just getting ready to head out, and I realized what time it is over there. Remember I asked you to pack a nice dress?"

Uh oh.

"Yes," I say.

"Well, I thought since you were alone tonight...."

I was right. He sent me out on some odd adventure he hopes will cure me of my heartache.

"Who is it?" I ask.

"Earl Mariner's son. Jason."

I rub my eyes. Peter tried once before to set me up with Jason, but Mom squashed the idea the minute it was suggested we meet. He was too old for me, she'd said.

"I don't know, Peter."

"It's just dinner, Mel. He's a law school student at UCLA, but he's studying in Paris for six months. He just got there about a week ago. Doesn't really know anybody yet. I was telling Earl last night about our trip, and he mentioned Jason was over there. I'm just worried about you being alone the next few days. I feel terrible."

"It's okay, really," I say. "I'm fine."

Peter doesn't respond, and I'm again sad for him. I don't know what it's like to have a dad, but I'm beginning to figure it out.

"Sure," I say. "I'll meet him."

"Great!" Peter replies. "He'll pick you up in the lobby of the hotel at seven o'clock."

We say goodbye and hang up.

I remove the black cocktail dress I packed from my suitcase and hang it in the bathroom while I shower, hoping the steam will loosen the wrinkles. Instead of pulling my hair away from my face, I leave it down. It keeps the scar on my cheek concealed a little. I apply my makeup, slip on my strappy black sandals, and stare at my reflection in the full-length mirror on the back of the bathroom door. I try to fill the emptiness with the kinds of thoughts a seventeen-year-old girl would have about meeting a UCLA law student in Paris for dinner, but I can't get Sam out of my head.

I walk into the hotel lobby just before seven o'clock. There are two women at the front desk, but nobody else is around. They look at me and smile, then whisper to one another before going back to whatever it is they're doing. In one corner of the lobby is a small lounge area with four plush chairs, two of them facing the front door of the hotel, the other two facing the bar. I decide to keep my back to the front door. That way, if Jason doesn't like what he sees through the glass, he can walk away without me noticing. If he has to come in and approach me from behind, before he has a chance to see my scars, he'll be less likely to run away.

The door to the hotel opens. My heart jumps into my throat. Shoes click across the tile floor.

"Bonjour," one of the women at the front desk says.

I hold my breath. Hands are resting on my shoulders. I stand up and turn around.

"Hello, Melanie," Sam says.

-26-

I exhale, slow and steady, and then pause before I take in another breath. The air moves fast into my lungs, so fast the sharpness of it startles me, and I stop breathing altogether.

"Sam?" I whisper.

I touch his cheek with the tips of my fingers, reassuring myself he's really standing in front of me. He places his hand over mine.

"Yes," he says. "It's me."

I step toward him, and he folds himself around me. My body melts into his. I rest my ear against his chest and listen to the steady rhythm of his heart as he runs his fingers through my hair before settling them on my cheek. His hand is warm. I inhale the smell of him and hold it, letting it fill all of the spaces in my body that were empty, until now.

"I'm so sorry, Melanie," he says.

I wrap my arms around his waist, the heat of his body moving through me and embracing me like someone who's been lost but is now found. The same woman who greeted Sam when he walked in the front door asks if he'd like his bag taken to the room. He nods.

"You're staying here?" I ask.

Sam smiles. "I hope so. That's what Peter planned."

"Peter?"

Sam leans forward, takes my face in his hands, and kisses me.

Peter was never coming to Paris. The day I talked to Steve, Sam returned my call, but I'd left my cell phone on the kitchen counter when I went to visit Donald Crowder. Peter came home, noticed ten missed calls from Sam on my phone, and when it rang again, he answered it. And they talked. And talked. And together, they came up with a plan to reunite us.

Sam and I spend five days exploring Paris together, visiting all of the highlighted sites in my travel book. On our last day, we stroll along the River Seine for hours talking about Joe and Mom and Kurt, reliving the day that took so much away from us. When I turned around in the lobby that first night in Paris and Sam was standing in front of me, I couldn't breathe. I was scared I might be dreaming. And when it finally settled over me that he was real, that he was actually there, I couldn't deny the anger that crept into my heart. I wanted to know why he'd hurt me. But then he held me, and I forgot everything because I knew it had nothing to do with me. We'd both needed that time and space to find our own ways through the pain, to reach an understanding of what had happened and to accept the possibility of moving forward.

Back in our room at the Hotel Duo, silvery-white light from a full moon dappled across our bed, Sam kisses my lips, then my neck. He moves slowly down my body, his fingers caressing my skin. We're both trembling as we slip out of our clothes, prepared this time to surrender our last bit of purity to one another. And when it happens, I hold him close to me, feel his tears mix with mine, and listen to the steady pulse of our hearts beating in tandem, as though our two souls have become one.

The following day, Sam catches his flight back to Kalispell, and I return to Los Angeles. But I only stay long enough to pack a new bag, this time one that will get me through a cold winter in Montana. After that, who knows?

The night before I leave, I visit Mom's grave again. I tell her about Sam and Paris, and I promise to come back when I return in the spring. I walk to the edge of the cliff as the sun meets the ocean, and as the water begins to wrap itself around that big orange ball of heat and light, I feel Mom standing next to me.

In the morning, Peter drives me to LAX. This time, he drops me off at the curb.

"Call me when you land," he says. "And call me again when you get to Steve's cabin."

"I will," I reply. "I promise."

He gives me a hug—a strong hug, a hug that tells me he loves me, that he's always loved me no matter how little he was able to show it in the past.

"I love you, Peter," I say.

"I love you too, Melanie."

On the flight to Salt Lake City, I watch through the window as concrete and steel and glass disappear behind us, replaced by suburban sprawl, then desert, and eventually, rolling green and yellow valleys that welcome us to Salt Lake. On the flight to Kalispell, the valleys transform into thick forest and rivers, and then those blue mountains appear below me, and I smile as we descend into Glacier International Airport.

Sam is leaning against the wall near the baggage carousel, his hands in the pockets of his jeans, his black hair tucked behind his ears. I run to him, and he catches me, and we kiss, longer and deeper than we've ever kissed before. He lifts me off the ground, and I bury my face in his neck, his strong arms holding me tight against his chest.

On the drive to Steve's cabin, he tells me Steve has gone to Chicago.

"We gave him an excuse to go," Sam says. "He didn't want to be a third leg. He packed as much stuff as he could in a backpack and took the train out of Whitefish. He'd saved about five grand. Said he'd check it out for a few months, and if things go well, he'll stay. If not, he'll come back." Sam smiles. "He got a ticket to a Bulls game on Saturday night. He wanted me to tell you he's sorry he didn't get to see you, but he couldn't miss the game."

I laugh as I imagine Steve on that train, walking away from his past and stepping into his future, maybe not knowing exactly what's in store for him in that future, but nevertheless being excited and scared at the same time. I wonder if we feel the same way, and then I wonder if this is how Mom felt when she climbed into the seat of that roller coaster.

That was the happiest day of my life, Melanie. Nobody could touch me.

In Columbia Falls, Sam turns left onto North Fork Road. We keep the windows of the truck rolled down. I rest my head on his shoulder and let the wind blow through my hair. It's warm and rich with the scent of pine needles and damp earth. Sam says cooler days are coming. I look forward to them. I've never seen real snow before.

At the cabin, he carries my suitcase into the second bedroom. I walk out onto the back deck and stare across the valley at the mountains in the distance, turning black beneath a rapidly setting sun. Below them is that winding, twisting river, its waters flowing endlessly. Forever.

Sam wraps his arms around my waist and pulls me to his chest. He kisses my ear, then my neck. Far off in the distance, two objects move back and forth across a sky turned crimson. I'm not sure if Sam sees them too, but then he points in their direction.

"Goldens," he says.

The eagles fly toward us, rising and falling, their wings moving in tandem like synchronized swimmers, and then they swoop into a nearby pine tree and land side by side, their eyes focused on Sam and me. He holds me a little tighter, and I squeeze his arms—a silent recognition and understanding of something we can't explain in words.

As the eagles lift their wings and return to flight, a warm breeze blows across my face, then quickly vanishes again, like a breath from God. I keep my eyes on the birds until they're nothing but black dots on the horizon…and then they're gone.

Acknowledgments

Many thanks to Crystal Patriarche and the team at BookSparks and SparkPress. It's been nothing but a pleasure working with you guys, and I'm forever grateful for your faith in my writing and your dedication to my work.

And to my parents, my brothers, and my amazing son, Jacob. Thank you for believing in me and for encouraging me to keep writing. But most of all, thank you for loving me!

About the Author

Fleur Philips is an award-winning author who holds a Master of Fine Arts in creative writing from Antioch University in Los Angeles and a Bachelor of Arts in English from the University of Montana. Her first novel, *I Am Lucky Bird,* was selected as a General Fiction Finalist for the 2011 Book of the Year Award from *ForeWord Reviews.* Her novel *Crumble* was named Young Adult Winner from the 2013 San Francisco Book Festival and was selected as a Young Adult Fiction Finalist by the 2013 International Book Awards. It was also awarded the Silver Medal in the Young Adult—Mature Issues category in the Moonbeam Children's Book Awards and was a Young Adult Fiction Finalist in the 2013 Best Book Awards from *USA Book News.* She lives in Whitefish, Montana with her son.

Connect with Fleur at www.fleurphilips.com, at Facebook.com/fleurphilipswriter, or on Twitter @fleurphilips.

About SparkPress

SparkPress is an independent boutique publisher delivering high-quality, entertaining, and engaging content that enhances readers' lives. We are proud of our catalog of both fiction and non-fiction titles, featuring authors who represent a wide array of genres, as well as our established, industry-wide reputation for innovative, creative, results-driven success in working with authors. SparkPress, a BookSparks imprint, is a division of SparkPoint Studio, LLC.

To learn more, visit us at www.sparkpointstudio.com.

CPSIA information can be obtained
at www.ICGtesting.com
Printed in the USA
FSOW02n0028290415
6772FS